MY PARENTS CANCELLED MY BIRTHDAY!

DISCARDED

Also by Jo Simmons

I Swapped My Brother on the Internet
The Dodo Made Me Do It

MY PARENTS CANCELLED MY BIRTHDAY!

Jo Simmons

illustrated by Nathan Reed

BLOOMSBURY
CHILDREN'S BOOKS
LONDON OXFORD NEW YORK NEW DELHI SYDNEY

BLOOMSBURY CHILDREN'S BOOKS
Bloomsbury Publishing Plc
50 Bedford Square, London WC1B 3DP, UK

BLOOMSBURY, BLOOMSBURY CHILDREN'S BOOKS and the Diana logo
are trademarks of Bloomsbury Publishing Plc

First published in Great Britain in 2019 by Bloomsbury Publishing Plc

A catalogue record for this book is available from the British Library

ISBN: PB: 978-1-5266-0658-7; ePub: 978-1-5266-0660-0

2 4 6 8 10 9 7 5 3 1

Typeset by RefineCatch Limited, Bungay, Suffolk

Printed and bound in Great Britain by CPI Group (UK) Ltd, Croydon CR0 4YY

To find out more about our authors and books visit www.bloomsbury.com
and sign up for our newsletters

For Mum, with love

CHAPTER ONE

THE FALL

It all started when a pig fell off the roof.

It wasn't just any old pig. It was our pig, Tiny.

Tiny was my sister Meg's pet pig. Tiny was a pygmy pig, which is a special kind of cute, small pig. At least, that's what the man we bought her from said. 'Oh yeah, she won't grow bigger than a pug,' he said. Only Tiny kept on growing.

1

Bigger than a pug.

Bigger than a spaniel.

Bigger than a Labrador.

Bigger and bigger and bigger, until she ended up regular pig size. And regular pigs are surprisingly BIG. They weigh a lot, too.

The hugeness of Tiny meant she couldn't live in our house, as Meg had planned, and the garden was too small. In the end, Dad decided to make a home for her on the garage roof. He built a fence around it and put a little pig house up there. Once a week, he'd climb through the bathroom window, on to the roof, and muck it off, which meant shovelling all the pig mess and old straw over the side.

This was Dad's least favourite job. He always swore while he was doing it, but using made-up words. This is something he does. He thinks not using real swear words makes him a Good Dad. If you were standing in the garden you'd hear him shouting **Branoch!** and **Zerk!** and other weird words. Only, thinking about it, you really wouldn't want to be standing in the garden as he shovelled the mess over the side. Too risky.

Anyway, it was a Sunday. A normal Sunday, or so I thought. How wrong.

We were all sitting out in the garden: me, Mum, Dad and Meg, plus my nana Maureen, with her tiny chihuahua dog, Margherita. Nana had recently dyed her hair again – blue this time, with purple tips. She had just come back from seeing Mystic Morris's show. Mystic Morris could talk to dead people. Someone in the audience would ask him to see if their dead uncle Bill was OK and he'd make contact with him and pass on a message. 'Bill says not to worry, he's fine and is wearing his favourite socks,' or something like that. Dad said it sounded like a load of **bippits** to him, and I thought he was right, but I didn't say anything.

The grown-ups were drinking tea and me and Meg were sitting on the grass, eating some of Nana's famous vegan carob cake. Dad says it could be used to repair motorway bridges after an earthquake, but it was all we had. Everything was normal. Normal, normal, fine, fine, fine, just a regular Sunday in August. My nana's been to see a psychic, my dad's teasing her using made-up swear words, great, fine, normal, then ... **crack!**

There was a crack.

Then ... **thud!**

There was a thud.

A big thud. In fact, a really massive **thud**.

We all jumped up in shock. Then Meg cried out, 'Tiny!'

That's what had caused the humungous thud sound. It was the sound of a huge pig falling off a roof.

We all rushed over. Everyone was shouting, 'Tiny, are you OK?' All of us except Nana. She was shouting, 'Margherita, where are you?'

I looked around. Margherita had vanished.

Had she run off, frightened by the falling pig?

Was she inside?

Out on the street?

Where could she be?

Where could she … And then we all had the same thought at exactly the same time. **Oh no!**

Mum looked at Dad, her eyes as wide as dinner plates. Dad muttered, **Spanjo**, Meg twizzled her hair nervously. Then Tiny stood up. Dad gasped. Nana shrieked.

Then ... **thud!**

Another thud, a bit less massive than the pig-falling thud, but still pretty big.

This was a Nana-falling thud.

So that's where Margherita was. She hadn't run away – worse luck for her. She had been on the patio and Tiny had fallen straight on her – a direct hit. What were the chances of that happening? But there was no time to puzzle that out. Nana had collapsed! Mum rushed to help and I saw Dad, spreading a large pair of pants that he'd pulled off the washing line over the exact spot on the patio where Tiny had crashed down.

Dad turned to me. 'Tom, find something

to put the dog in, for goodness sake,' he said. 'Something big enough to take a two-dimensional chihuahua.'

'What?' I said, confused.

'For Margherita!' he said. 'She's completely flattened. I need a box or something to put her in.'

I had never been asked to find a container for a squashed dog before. It threw me a bit, I'll be honest. I quickly searched the kitchen cupboards: ice cream containers, sandwich boxes ... Nothing was right. **Curses!** I ran up to my room and emptied Lego from an old shoebox.

'Will this do?' I asked Dad, giving him the box. He tried to get flattened Margherita into the box. I looked away, but I could tell he was struggling. He was swearing quietly again and sweating.

'**Zablash!**' he said. 'Too small. We need something wider. The dog's as flat as a pancake. You wouldn't think a chihuahua could spread so far.'

I ran back inside. I checked the recycling. Perfect – an old takeaway pizza box.

'Perfect,' said Dad. 'An old takeaway pizza box.'

As Dad put the dog into the pizza box, I realised that we had actually had a margherita pizza in that box. And now there was Margherita the dog in that box. This is known as ironic. I didn't say anything.

Dad handed me the box.

'Get rid of it,' he said.

I had never been asked to do that before either; to get rid of a squashed dog. There was nowhere in the garden I could bury a box that size – the garden was too small and mostly patio.

I ran out into the street. That's when I had an idea. There was a nursery at the end of the road. It was shut for the summer holidays. Great. I hopped over the fence and buried the box in the sandpit. Nice and deep. By the time the kids were back in September, it would all be long gone.

I sprinted back to my house. There was an ambulance outside. The ambulance men were helping Nana into the back of it. She reached out to me. 'My baby!'

I had never been called that by Nana before. Maybe she had banged her head.

'Yes, yes, I'm your baby,' I said, trying to be nice and calm.

'Where is my baby?' she wailed.

Then I got it. She was talking about

Margherita. I didn't know what to say. I couldn't tell the truth – Margherita's in a pizza box, in the sandpit at Bright Futures nursery. That would definitely upset her.

So I said nothing. The ambulance doors shut. The blue lights came on. It drove away.

Then I was aware of something short standing close to me – my sister, Meg.

'Look,' said Meg, holding up a small white thing. 'My tooth's come out.'

CHAPTER TWO

DEAD DOG DISASTERS

So that was Sunday. A day of drama and disaster and lots of Dad's made-up swear words.

Luckily, Monday started out better. Mum went to work. Dad shut himself in the dining room. Only you had to call it the study, and you weren't allowed in if the

DO NOT DISTURB,

WRITER AT WORK

sign was up. Dad was writing his book.

Dad had been writing his book for a long time. Years. He said it was nearly finished though. Everyone was excited about this, especially Mum. She hoped Dad's book would be a bestseller so she could stop working so hard to pay the bills while Dad worked on his book and earned zero money.

The house was nice and quiet and that suited me fine. I had a very important job to do. Something was coming; something was just five days away. Something very, very, very important indeed.

MY BIRTHDAY!!

Super exciting! In fact, beyond exciting! I know, I know, everyone gets excited about their birthday, but mine is different. Here are the facts:

1. It is right at the end of the summer holidays. Which means I am the youngest in my year at school. And which also means that every year I have to wait, and wait, and wait for my birthday, while all my friends have theirs one after another, before me. Bah!

2. Some people even have birthdays in September, right at the start of the school year, so they get to go first with all the birthday fuss, and no one is ever away on summer holiday to spoil things like they are with my August birthday.

3. These September birthday people include Chas Cheeseman. He is the oldest in our year. He had, I have to admit, an amazing party last September for his eleventh birthday. There were fireworks, a personal chef who made anything you wanted

to eat (I had an ice cream and doughnut sandwich, while Harry, aka the Hulk because he is freakishly big for his age, had custard and chips). Then, at the end, we all got given a drone. Not a slice of cake wrapped in a bit of kitchen roll. A drone! It was seriously amazing, although I slightly hate to admit it. Annoyingly, it was so amazing that everyone was *still* talking about it, nearly a year later!

And on the last day of term, before we broke up for summer, Chas was already talking about his next birthday – and I hadn't even had mine yet!

But finally it was August. Finally it was my turn to have a birthday. Finally my turn to be eleven. I felt like I had waited **FOREVER** for this moment.

I wanted my birthday party to be the best, most exciting one ever.

Better than Chas Cheeseman's.

I wanted people to talk about my birthday for even longer than a year afterwards – two years; even three! I wanted them to say, 'Chas's eleventh birthday was fun, but what about Tom's? Now *that* was a seriously awesome day. That's how you do a birthday!'

As luck would have it, this year was

also my **LUCKY BIRTHDAY**. It's a Bostock family tradition. Your Lucky Birthday is when your age matches your birthdate. My birthday is 11th August and this year I am eleven on 11th August. My Lucky Birthday! Meg had already had her lucky birthday. She was only four then and I was six. We can't remember a lot about it, because we were only small, but we definitely remember it was a big deal, with extra presents, tons of food, decorations and non-stop fun. And now it was finally my turn. I just knew it was going to be amazing. I couldn't think about anything else!

'There was bunting, wasn't there?' said Meg.

I was drawing birthday party invitations in Meg's room. I sometimes hung out in here. Her room was bigger than mine. Meg was colouring in her tooth, the one that came out yesterday, using a green pen. Apparently, the tooth fairy had not turned up last night, so she was making it more eye-catching. We were trying to remember what a Lucky Birthday involved.

'Yeah, but then Harry tried to swing on it and pulled it all down,' I said.

Meg laughed.

'There was a big cake, too, which somebody fell in, I think,' I said. 'I really want a big cake for my Lucky Birthday. Chas Cheeseman's had three levels, and sweets all spilt out when you cut into it.'

I worked hard on the invitations. All morning, in fact.

They had to be good.

Everything had to be good.

I had done one for my best friend, Keith, and for Harry the Hulk and also for Jonny. He was quite a new friend. I got to know him last year after he became famous in my school for trying to swap his brother on the internet. It didn't work out, but that's another story.

I planned to design a particularly amazing invitation for Chas, using fluorescent pens and glitter, but first I needed lunch. Dad made it. Dad does most of the cooking in our house. He's a really good cook. Mum loves his food, but worries Dad spends too much time cooking and not enough time finishing his book. Dad says Mum is a terrible cook, so he has no choice.

After lunch, while I was busy working on Chas's invitation, the doorbell rang. It was Nana. She had come home from hospital in a taxi. She had a walking stick. She had banged her hip when she fell over in shock yesterday. It wasn't broken, just bruised, but she needed to live with us until she was properly better. Then she said:

'Where is she?'

'Who, Jill?' said Dad (Jill is another name for Mum). 'At work, as usual.'

'No! Margherita, my baby!' said Nana.

'Oh, right, yes,' said Dad. 'She's gone, I'm afraid.'

Gone where? I wondered. Then I remembered the sandpit at Bright Futures nursery. And I also remembered people sometimes say 'gone' when they mean 'dead'.

Nana shook her head. Her blue-with-purple-tips hair flicked about. She started limping through the house, stroking the walls and sniffing the air. She said she'd seen Mystic Morris, the man who could talk to dead people, do something similar during his show.

Suddenly Nana gasped and spread her arms wide. Her walking stick thwacked Dad on the chest and he made an 'oof' sound.

'She's here!' cried Nana.

And then …

'She's gone!' cried Meg, running in from the garden.

CHAPTER THREE

GONE

Wow, now Meg is saying 'gone' instead of 'dead', I thought.

But then Nana blurted out: 'She hasn't gone! She is here. I can sense her presence. I FEEL her. Listen! Was that her yapping? Shhhhh.'

Meg grabbed my ear and yanked it to her mouth, and said urgently: 'Not Margherita. Tiny! **TINY HAS GONE!**'

Tiny!

We had all forgotten about Tiny. What with Margherita getting squashed, Nana collapsing, me burying the pizza box in the sandpit at Bright Futures nursery, the ambulance and Meg's tooth coming out, we forgot about the pig.

But of course she'd gone. Pigs are quite intelligent. I expect she sensed the trouble she was in, having just totalled Nana's beloved dog, and she legged it. I felt a surge of respect for Tiny in that moment.

'Where is she?' said Meg, waggling another wobbly tooth nervously. 'Where is Tiny? She is my pig. I miss her. Where are you, Tiny?'

'Where are you, Margherita?' wailed Nana.

And where was Dad? Then I noticed the dining-room door – I mean study door – clicking shut with the

DO NOT DISTURB, WRITER AT WORK

sign hanging on it.

Great!

My sister is crying about a lost pig.

My nana is sure that her dead dog is somehow haunting the house.

My dad has snuck off back to his dining-study to work on his book, and as usual it was left to me to sort things out when all I wanted to do is finish my birthday party invitations. **Curses!** Didn't anyone realise how important that was?

I made everyone sit down.

I promised Meg I would go out and look for Tiny.

'And buy some Nosho Liver & Spleen, too,' said Nana.

I promised Nana I would buy some dog

food, too. I didn't point out that dead dogs don't need to eat dog food, or any food, any more.

I went out.

I bought some Nosho Liver & Spleen, that was fine, but I couldn't find Tiny.

How far can a pig walk in a day? You might think not far, but it is far. It must be.

I checked the park. I checked near the big wheelie bin outside the Co-op where Tiny might have been eating scraps. I knocked on Harry the Hulk's door in case Tiny had gone there.

Nothing.

I went home.

Meg was upset when I told her Tiny was still missing. I suggested we make some

HAVE YOU SEEN THIS PIG?

posters to put up round the neighbourhood.

'But let's do them quickly, Meg,' I said. 'I need to get all my party invites done this afternoon, so I can deliver them first thing tomorrow.'

Then Nana called us into the kitchen. She had put some little portions of Nosho Liver & Spleen into saucers.

'Go and put these on the floor – one in each room at least. And don't forget the entrance hall,' she said.

'What for?' said Meg.

'For Margherita. She is here. In the house. Her spirit remains here. We must feed her.'

There was really no answer to this.

Even Meg realised that.

We just did as we were told, then ran upstairs to get on with our art projects: the very-soon-and-important-birthday-related art and the missing-pig-related art.

Next thing we knew, it was the evening and Mum was home from work and had even made dinner, too. Unusual.

Dad came out of his dining-study and immediately stepped in a saucer of Nosho Liver & Spleen, which made him shout, **'Menarcho!'**

I helped Nana to the table – she was still limping – and Mum served us all spaghetti bolognese. All except Nana, who didn't eat meat and was having something Mum called vegetable surprise. The surprise was there were no vegetables in it – it was just a bowl of spaghetti.

'So, how was everybody's day?' Mum asked.

'Tiny has gone,' said Meg.

'And Margherita is here,' said Nana.

Mum looked confused.

'Don't be alarmed. It's wonderful,' said

Nana. 'I feel reassured by her spirit presence. She lives on within these walls. But I must care for her and feed her.'

'So that's why there's dog food on the floor,' said Dad, pointing at his sock.

Mum sighed quietly.

'Speaking of food, why don't we eat?' she said.

Dad took a mouthful, Meg sucked a long strand of spaghetti up and I shovelled in a spoonful of sauce and then, all at once, like we'd planned it to the exact second, we all spat our food out on to our plates.

'**Yannicks!**' yelled Dad.

'Yuck,' shouted Meg, making a face like a cat coughing up a furball.

'What?' said Mum. Then she raised her fork to her mouth.

'**NOOOOO!!**'

we all shouted.

Too late. She popped it in. Her cheeks went pale. Her eyebrows shot up! And yes, she spat it out.

'Appalling, isn't it?' said Dad. 'What did you put in it?'

'I used that mince in the fridge,' said Mum.

'What mince in the fridge?' said Dad.

'The stuff in a tin,' said Mum.

'Mince doesn't come in a tin,' said Dad.

'No, but Nosho Liver & Spleen does,' I said, my hand flying up to my mouth.

CHAPTER FOUR

TROUBLE WITH THE TOOTH FAIRY

The next day it was Tuesday, the day that always follows Monday.

There were now just four days to go until my birthday. After waiting so long for it, it was very nearly here. And because it was my Lucky Birthday, I still didn't really know what was going to happen. I was sure Mum and

Dad had arranged all kinds of cool things in secret, but I had some questions anyway. Like:

1. Could my best friend, Keith, stay over the night before my birthday as well as on my birthday?
2. Could I open my presents at 6 a.m.?
3. Could I have waffles for breakfast with extra syrup and ice cream, but no fruit?

I asked Mum all this as soon as I got up, but she said, 'I don't have time to talk about this now, Tom, I'll be late for work.'

Nana paid no attention to my questions either. She was sitting on the sofa, consulting crystals about Margherita's exact location. She kept sighing and saying she couldn't get a clear message.

After breakfast, I went out to deliver the

invitations to my birthday party. Meg came along. She asked where her invitation was. This was a bit awkward. I wanted to use her bedroom for a sleepover – my friends wouldn't all fit in my room. But I wanted Meg to go and stay at Nana's for the night. Eleven was too old to have your little sister at your party. Chas Cheeseman hadn't let his sister be at his. So I said nothing.

We delivered the invitations and then got on with putting up the **HAVE YOU SEEN THIS PIG?** posters.

At the cafe in the park, we asked Bruce, the owner, if we could put up a pig poster inside. Bruce read the poster slowly.

'So how will I know if it's your pig?' he asked.

'If you see a pig, it's probably ours,' I said. 'I mean, how many pigs do you see wandering around usually?'

'But does it answer to its name? Does it have any special markings?'

'It's just a pig!' I said.

'Should I approach the pig if I see it?' Bruce asked. 'I could give it some food. A bacon sandwich, maybe?'

A bacon sandwich?

To a pig?

I sighed.

'If you see a pig, Bruce, any pig at all, please just call us,' I said.

Bruce agreed, then made us each a bacon sandwich. I demolished mine, then noticed that Meg had hardly touched hers.

'Don't you want your sandwich, Meg?' I asked.

She pushed it across the table to me.

We spent another hour or so putting up the last of the pig posters, and then walked home. I was busy thinking about additional presents to add to my birthday list when suddenly Meg said:

'I think it's because of me.'

'What?' I said.

'Margherita getting squashed and Tiny running away. My tooth fell out at exactly the same time. And then there was no money from the tooth fairy under my pillow the next day. She must be mad at me! Every time a tooth falls out, bad things happen to us. It's the curse of the tooth fairy!'

I didn't know what to say. I tried to tell Meg that there was no link between her tooth falling out and all the stuff that had just happened. That in fact her tooth fell out just *after* Tiny fell off the roof and squashed Margherita. She wasn't having it.

'I must make sure no more of my teeth drop out,' she said.

'Don't be daft, Meg!' I said. 'Wobbly teeth are normal. It's nature giving you a second chance at cutting back on sugar. You get a whole set of baby teeth free that you can mess up, before you have to get serious and look after the grown-up ones.'

This dental wisdom was wasted on Meg. She had her hand over her mouth, but I could just hear her saying: 'I have a wobbly tooth right now, but it must never fall out. Ever! Or who knows what might happen?'

We had reached home. Meg ran straight to her room and I went to mine. I wanted to do some research into the extra presents I'd just thought of, so I could put them on my list.

Later, I went down to the kitchen, expecting to find Dad making dinner. Instead, Nana was sitting at the table, which was covered in a thick black cloth. The curtains were drawn and Nana had draped floaty scarves from the clothes airer that hung above the table. It was slightly spooky.

'We're having a séance,' she said.

'A say what?'

CHAPTER FIVE

ARE YOU THERE, MARGHERITA?

How to explain what a séance is …

A séance is when people try to make contact with the dead. A bit like what Mystic Morris does, only you can do it at home, round the kitchen table. Not that many people ever do, because, obviously, it's weird and creepy, and also stupid.

It was Nana's idea, of course. She believed Margherita was in distress; that her spirit was not quiet. She wanted to speak with Margherita. And for speak, I mean 'speak', when you put your fingers up and do little quote marks around the word to show you don't mean it. How can you speak with a dead dog, after all? You can't even speak with a live one.

When Mum got in from work she wasn't too keen on the idea of a séance either.

'What will Margherita tell you anyway, Mum?' she asked Nana.

'If she is OK. If she is at rest. And where her body is. None of you will tell me. Lewis just says she is buried.' (Lewis is another name for Dad.)

I felt myself going a bit pale. What if Margherita told Nana that she was in the sandpit at Bright Futures nursery? Then I realised this was ridiculous. There was no way Nana was going to find that out. Least of all from a dead dog.

We spread our hands on the table and touched little fingers.

'Your hands are shaking a bit, Tom,' said Dad, then he whispered, 'Don't worry, this is just a load of old **bajinders**, son.'

Nana lit a candle and put it in the middle of the black tablecloth. She started to hum softly. Then she said:

'If you're there, Margherita, flicker the flame.'

The flame flickered.

Just a draught, surely.

'Are you all right, Margherita? Flicker the flame once for yes, twice for no.'

We hardly moved, hardly breathed. We watched the candle. Nothing, nothing,

nothing … Then it flickered – twice!

'Oh, my darling,' said Nana. 'You're not at rest.'

The flame flickered again. That must have been Dad breathing out. It certainly wasn't me. I was holding my breath.

'Can you tell me where you are?' Nana asked.

No one dared move.

'Are you buried underground?'

We stared at the flame, hardly breathing. It twitched once – yes.

'Are you buried near this house?'

Silence for ages. I stared so hard at the flame that the room seemed to disappear. It twitched once again – yes.

'Are you buried …'

BING BONG!

The doorbell! We all shrieked. Meg grabbed

her teeth. Mum grabbed me. Nana clutched her chest and Dad shot up out of his chair and smashed his head on the metal clothes airer, draped in scarves, above the table.

'**Owwwwww,**' he yelled, rubbing his head.

One of the scarves drifted down and caught alight in the candle. It started burning really fast, and then the tablecloth caught on fire, too! Nana leaped up and hid in the corner while Mum tried to beat the flames out with an apron.

That didn't work, so she ran upstairs to get a bath towel, shoving Dad out of the way, who stubbed his toe on one of the chairs. He began hopping around, holding on to his foot with one hand and his head with the other, swearing, but this time in actual English. I won't repeat what he said.

BING BONG!

The doorbell went again. Mum rushed into the room with a towel and started beating the fire with it. Sparks flew up and Nana started whimpering about 'the end of the world'. Then the smoke alarm started, a high-pitched wee-wee-wee that made Dad grab his head even tighter.

BING BONG!

The doorbell. Again!

As no adults were available to answer the door, I went.

It was a police officer. Which was bad. He was holding a pizza takeaway box that definitely had sand on it. Which was super extra bad.

'Some children at the summer school down at Bright Futures dug this up,' he said. 'They were highly upset when they saw what was inside. I won't open it, but suffice to say it contains the remains of a flat chihuahua. A flat chihuahua which has a pet microchip. We scanned it and the animal is registered to a Mrs Maureen Fennel. Her neighbours informed us that she is currently residing in this very property. May I speak with her?'

Thinking fast, I said, 'No.'

The policeman frowned. Then I confessed everything.

'It was me, Officer, that put the dog there. I just needed to bury her quickly so my nana didn't get upset. I didn't realise there would be children there at summer school. I'm really sorry. I won't do it again. I promise.'

'How did the dog get so flat?' the police officer asked. 'Looks like it was run over by a steamroller.'

'A pig, actually. It didn't run the dog over, it fell on it and squashed it.'

The police officer was silent for a moment. He looked confused.

'Hmm, right, well, make sure you bury the dog in a sensible place this time,' he said. 'And not on public property. I could have you in court for less.'

Then he glanced past me and saw the smoke and Dad hopping around holding his head and his foot. I glanced too. It looked like Mum had put the fire out.

'Everything all right in there?' he asked.

'Yes, fine, thank you, we were just having a séance.'

He frowned, and then nodded and left. I went back inside, carrying the box. Dad was now lying on the sofa, Mum was opening windows to let the smoke out and Nana was still in the corner of the kitchen, just sort of standing there in a daze.

I would have to try and bury the pizza box in the garden after all, but not right now. Too many witnesses. So I did the only thing I could think to do. I put it in the freezer.

Once safely inside, I leaned against the freezer door and shut my eyes for a second. Phew! Then I felt someone tugging my sleeve. I opened my eyes. It was Meg. She was holding up something small and white. Her face was also small and white. Very white.

'My tooth fell out!' she whispered. 'Then Dad hurt his head and the house nearly burned down. It's all my fault. The tooth fairy. **She has cursed me!**'

CHAPTER SIX

THE BIRTHDAY BOMB IS DROPPED

Dad spent the night on the sofa. He said his head hurt if he moved. He still had a headache the next morning. Bright light made it worse, so we closed all the curtains. But that made the house very dark and explains why Mum stepped in a saucer of Nosho Liver & Spleen.

Mum was upstairs changing her socks

while I made breakfast. I put some bread in the toaster for myself, but Meg didn't want any. She refused to eat any food with texture.

'I can't let any more teeth fall out,' she said, squishing cornflakes in milk with a fork. 'The curse! Remember?'

She looked pale and anxious, but I couldn't help thinking more about my birthday. Only three days to go! THREE DAYS!!

Nana said the fire had frightened off the spirit of Margherita. She said the communication with her had gone cold. That's not the only thing that's gone cold when it comes to Margherita, I thought, remembering the pizza box in the freezer.

Frankly, cold communication was fine by me. The sooner Nana stopped leaving dog food around and moved back to her own flat, the better. I needed the house to be normal, not haunted, for my birthday. My birthday was my day; the one day of the year that was about me; the one day I'd been looking forward to for ages and ages and ages.

The toast popped up and I started spreading butter on it. I thought about what exciting activities my parents might have planned for it, what amazing food Dad would cook, what special presents they might have bought. Meg carried on mashing her cornflakes. Then Mum came in, looking for her car keys, which wasn't easy, because it was so dark.

'Have you ordered my cake yet, Mum?' I asked her. 'Can it have sweets inside it like Chas Cheeseman's?'

Mum was still rushing about, trying to find her keys.

'Can you give me a clue, just a little clue,

about what we'll be doing on my birthday?' I asked her.

Mum stopped suddenly in front of me.

'Tom, hang on a minute,' she said. 'Are you aware of what's been going on here over the last few days? I mean, are you?'

I squinted at her in the dim light, my knife in mid-air.

'There's just too much happening right now,' she said. 'What with Dad's bad head and me having to work extra hours at the office and Nana thinking that Margherita is haunting the house and Tiny missing and, you know, everything. I just can't think about your birthday now.'

'Keep the noise down,' moaned Dad from the sofa.

'That's fine, we can talk about it tonight when you get in from work,' I said. This sounded pretty sensible and grown-up to me. I was a tiny bit proud of myself.

'No, Tom, you're not listening,' Mum spluttered. 'I don't think we can do your birthday.'

The knife dropped from my hand. It made a loud clattering noise against the plate.

'**Ninocks!** My *head*!' moaned Dad.

'What do you mean, we can't **"do"** my birthday?' I said. 'It's a thing, it's about to happen, I was born nearly eleven years ago. It can't just not exist. You can't just not do it. It's my day, it's my Lucky—'

'I'm sorry, Tom,' Mum interrupted.

I was beginning to shake. Meg stopped mashing her cornflakes. Silence.

'Wait!' I said. 'Are you cancelling my birthday?'

Mum shrugged and sighed.

'No, just postponing it,' she said. 'Putting

it off, for a bit. That's all. We'll do it later – in September or October. When Dad doesn't have a bad head and the ghost of Margherita has gone and … Lewis, back me up here.'

Dad limped into the kitchen, one hand on his forehead.

'Sorry, Tom, it's for the best,' he muttered. 'Your mum's right. We'll do your birthday later.'

Then he limped back to the sofa. Like he hadn't just ruined my life.

'But Mum, Dad – you can't do a birthday later,' I shouted, jumping to me feet. 'It's a day. A single day. The day of your birth. The day after my birthday is not my birthday. The day a week after my birthday is also not my birthday. All the days in September and October are not my birthdays. Not one of them. There is only one birthday. The eleventh of August. And if we don't do my birthday on my birthday, then you are, basically, cancelling my birthday.'

Then Mum said what she always says. 'I don't have time to talk about this now, I'll be late for work.'

Then she grabbed the keys, which were in the fruit bowl on the table all along, and walked out.

I ran after her into the hallway. Too late. The front door slammed. She was gone.

My knees gave way. I slumped to the floor, and sat straight in a bowl of Nosho Liver & Spleen. It squelched through my shorts. This is what having your birthday cancelled feels like. Like you've sat in dog food. Which I actually had. But even if I hadn't, it would have felt like this.

I was too stunned to get up. The dog food was cold and wet, but still I couldn't move.

How had it come to this?

WHO CANCELS THEIR SON'S BIRTHDAY!?!

Their son's Lucky Birthday!

Eventually, I found the strength to go upstairs and shut myself in my bedroom.

Meg tapped lightly on the door a little later and came in.

'Are you OK?' she asked. 'It's so awful about your birthday. I think it's my fault. The tooth-fairy curse!'

'I've been looking forward to this birthday for so long,' I moaned. 'Everyone else has had theirs, and finally it's my turn, and it's my Lucky Birthday as well, and I just wanted one day, just one day to be fun and amazing and mine. And now, this ...'

Meg sat there in silence. I lost track of time. A bit later, Meg bought me some Jaffa Cakes and then left me to my thoughts.

After the Jaffa Cakes and more lying on my bed feeling miserable, I rang my best friend, Keith. I needed to speak to someone. Keith is an unusual name and Keith is an unusual guy. Apparently, it was popular a few decades ago but has since mostly died out. Like DVDs.

'Hi, Keith. You'll never believe this. It's a disaster. My parents cancelled my birthday!'

'Who is this?' said Keith.

I gave Keith a strong look, which of course he couldn't see, because we were on our phones.

'It's Tom, your best friend.'

'Oh, hi, Tom, how are you?' he said.

'My parents cancelled my birthday.'

'Whoa! Can they do that?'

'I don't know, but they have.'

'What are you going to do?' Keith asked.

'First I need to get up and change my clothes,' I said. 'I sat in some dog food.'

'Good,' said Keith.

'Then I need time to think. What would you do if your parents cancelled your birthday?'

'Tricky ...' said Keith. He was quiet for a while. I thought he was thinking. Then I realised he was chewing some toast. Finally, he said:

'Well, Mr Connors at school always goes on about Resistingance, doesn't he? Which means fighting back. Like a warrior.'

'Resilience,' I said. 'Mr Connors goes on about resilience. Which means being strong and not flaking out. I think.'

'OK, well, you could do either,' said Keith. 'Resistingance or the other one. At least you've got some choices.'

'Thanks, Keith, I'm going to take a shower,' I said. 'I can't do either while I stink of Nosho Liver & Spleen.'

'Does this mean I can keep your present?'

I hung up.

CHAPTER SEVEN

RESISTINGANCE!

After my shower, I got back into my pyjamas and went to bed. I lay there for most of the morning. I think I was in shock. My parents cancelled my birthday. My Lucky Birthday. Does it get any more shocking than that? No, it doesn't.

To make things worse, everyone ignored me. Mum was at work. Dad had his headache on the sofa. Meg was too busy worrying about her tooth-fairy curse. Nana didn't even try to make it upstairs to check on me. I know she had a bad hip (although, thinking back to yesterday, she *did* jump up pretty quickly when the fire broke out ...) and I know she was sad about Margherita dying, but it would have been nice to see her. Or anyone really.

My birthday was cancelled, the one I had looked forward to for so long. Gone. Over. Not happening.

Then I remembered I had already sent the invitations out. What would Chas Cheeseman say when I told him it was cancelled? This was doubly, triply awful, plus also miserable, sad and really embarrassing. And just awful again.

I went downstairs. It was very dark. I could just make out Dad slumbering on the sofa with a flannel on his face.

'Dad,' I whispered.

He sprang up in shock. The flannel fell into his lap. Then he clutched his head and moaned.

'You **niblitz!**' he swore. 'My headache was just beginning to ease, then you go and scare the **blethers** out of me! What are you playing at, Tom?'

'I just wanted to check if you were still cancelling my birthday,' I said.

Dad groaned, lay down again and covered his face.

'It is my Lucky Birthday,' I said. 'You know, if you absolutely have to cancel a birthday, could you cancel next year's instead? I really, really want this birthday, this year. Can I? Please?'

Dad still said nothing.

'That's a no, then, is it?' I asked.

No answer.

I went into the kitchen. Nana was sitting at the table with her eyes closed.

'My parents cancelled my birthday, Nana,' I sighed.

'Shush, I'm meditating,' she said. 'I need to clear my mind of worry and be open and ready for the next time Margherita speaks to me.'

I found Meg in her room. She was sticking Blu-Tack around her teeth.

She said something. I think it was: 'So no more teeth fall out. Can't risk another family disaster.' But her mouth was so full it was hard to tell. She was dribbling a bit, too.

'Believe me, Meg, the tooth fairy has nothing to do with anything. Sticking Blu-Tack around your teeth will not make Mum and Dad uncancel my birthday. They have CANCELLED MY BIRTHDAY, remember?'

She nodded frantically and pointed at her mouth. She said something like, 'I mow, mam mits da curds!'

I felt like giving up. I wanted to cry. Maybe I did cry, I can't be sure.

I went back to bed. Hours passed. My mind, normally so sharp and smart, had gone to mush, like Meg's soupy cornflakes. I couldn't think straight. I couldn't move. It was like the weight of having my birthday cancelled was pinning me to the bed. Maybe this was how Margherita felt when Tiny landed on her?

Then I got a text from Keith.

DID YOU CHOOSE RESILIENCE OR RESISTINGANCE? FROM KEITH.

So far, I had chosen nothing. I had chosen bed and pyjamas and sadness, never-ending sadness.

Maybe, though, Keith had a point.

Maybe I did have choices.

Maybe rather than just putting up with having my birthday cancelled and being resilient, I needed to get some of Keith's Resistingance going. I needed to fight back! It all became clear. There was no point sulking. If I wanted to have my birthday, I had to make it happen myself.

I sat up in bed, my heart beating fast.

Suddenly I felt alive. ALIVE! Not dead, like a chihuahua under a gigantic pig. Alive, like a nice, clean almost-eleven-year-old boy who didn't smell of Nosho Liver & Spleen any more and deserved the very best from life!

It wouldn't be easy, but I saw what I had to do. Having a brilliant birthday, as good as Chas Cheeseman's birthday had been, was not about begging my parents to uncancel my birthday. I had to do more. I had to make my own luck. If I wanted my Lucky Birthday to happen at all, first I had to fix my family.

I made a list:

1. Convince Meg that she is no longer cursed by the tooth fairy.
2. Fix Dad's headaches so he can get back to finishing his book.
3. Persuade Mum to work less (see above).

4. Persuade Nana to stop looking for dead Margherita and go back to her flat.

This wasn't going to be easy. One almost-eleven-year-old boy, three days and a whole load of mess to put right. I wasn't sure where to begin.

My phone rang.

A quiet, friendly voice on the end of the line said: 'I think I've found your pig.'

It was a good start.

CHAPTER EIGHT

PIG, CHICKENS, PLAN

Tiny! Found at last, by a nice-sounding man called Mr Hector. He described the pig to me – very large, fond of apples – and I knew, right away, it was Tiny.

I rushed downstairs. Meg was squashing a banana through a sieve in the kitchen.

'I'm just making it nice and soft. I must not lose any more teeth.'

There was nothing to say to this. I just shook my head and ran out of the door.

Mr Hector lived nearby, with a huge garden tucked away behind houses. You would never guess it was there. While we had an OK house with a tiny garden, Mr Hector had a tiny house – more of a shed really – and a massive garden. It was full of trees and plants, bushes and bees and chickens. Lots of chickens. They all rushed over to me when I arrived and followed me around, clucking. It was a bit distracting.

Mr Hector was sitting under an apple tree. Tiny was lying at his feet. She looked happy. There were no signs that she had recently fallen off a roof. I scratched her ear. She grunted. The chickens clucked and hopped about by my feet.

'I better take her home,' I said. 'Thank you

for looking after her. My sister will be really glad to see her again.'

Maybe Meg would be so pleased to see Tiny that she'd forget about the crazy tooth-fairy curse, stop eating mashed cornflakes and sieved bananas, stop stuffing Blu-Tack in her face and get back to normal. And I'd be one step closer to having a functioning family again, ready to celebrate my birthday.

Then I remembered Nana.

She would not be pleased to see Tiny again. Tiny was, after all, the reason her chihuahua died. Tiny was a murderer.

'Where do you keep this here pig?' Mr Hector asked.

'On the garage roof,' I said.

'Roof's no place for a pig of this size. She needs grass, space, a pig house.'

Mr Hector had a point. Plus, I suddenly

realised, Dad hadn't fixed the fence. It wasn't safe for Tiny to go back up there. She'd fall straight off again, crushing who knows what this time.

More problems!

Problems that were getting in the way of my attempts at Resistingance, family fixing and birthday uncancelling. **Arrgghh!**

I sat down on the grass and told Mr Hector everything. I hadn't planned to tell him everything, but it just all came out – how Tiny had fallen off the roof, crushed Margherita, the séance, the tooth-fairy curse and how my parents had cancelled my birthday. Two chickens sat in my lap and fell asleep as I talked.

Mr Hector sucked on his pipe for a moment.

'I can't make your parents change their minds about your birthday,' he said. 'But I can look after the pig for you. She can stay here until things are fixed. You can come and see her whenever you like.'

That was helpful. I was really glad for that little bit of helpful. I thanked Mr Hector, patted Tiny and got up to leave. The chickens followed me to the gate.

'WAIT!' Mr Hector shouted from under the tree. 'Lift up your right arm.'

I turned around. 'My what, sorry?'

'Your right arm.'

As I lifted my right arm, all the chickens lifted their right wings, as if following my command. Mr Hector laughed and scratched his head.

'Well I'll be,' he said. 'You're a chicken whisperer! A chicken whisperer, as I live and breathe.'

You can say 'chicken whisperer' as many times as you like, I thought, but I've still got no idea what you're talking about. Mr Hector seemed to sense my confusion.

'A chicken whisperer can communicate with chickens,' he said. 'And not just with words, but through gestures and even thoughts. It's a rare power, son. You should be proud.'

I didn't really feel proud to be a chicken whisperer. I didn't even want to be a chicken whisperer. I certainly hadn't expected to discover that I was, in fact, a chicken whisperer. Not today and not ever. It was not on my birthday present list and it was not on my family-fixing to-do list. It would be more helpful to be a parent whisperer. But all the same, I thanked Mr Hector anyway, and ran home.

Back at the house, I wanted to tell Meg I had found Tiny safe and well. I thought she'd be pleased, but I found her sticking tape around her teeth.

'I just need to keep hold of my teeth,' she said. 'No crunchy food (but also no Blu-Tack, it tastes disgusting) and just wait for the curse to be lifted.'

'Which is when, exactly?' I asked. 'My birthday is three days away! Actually, more like two and a bit now! TWO AND A BIT!!'

'I don't know!' said Meg, twiddling a curl of hair nervously. 'It's up to the tooth fairy to lift the curse.'

'How will you know when she's done that?' I asked, feeling very frustrated by Meg's lack of logic.

'When she tells me, I suppose, and leaves some money under my pillow again. There has been no money for either of my teeth that just fell out. Then I'll know.'

Great. So now there were two members of my family waiting to hear from a dead and/or mythical creature. Meg was sounding dangerously similar to Nana now. I had to do something — and fast! I thought about Resistingance again. And that's when **The Plan** popped into my head.

I went to my room and I rang Keith.

'Hi, Keith, it's me.'

'Who?' he said.

'It's Tom, your best friend. Are you free tonight? I've got a little job for you.'

'What, like a bank job?' said Keith. 'Are you robbing a bank? Cool.'

'No, I just need someone fairly short, like you, to do some acting.'

'Oh sorry, no, I can't,' said Keith. 'I have to help my cousin Craig. It's pie-making night tonight. Happens once a month. I can't miss it.'

Then he hung up.

I'd have to ask Harry instead, even though he was massively tall and not exactly ideal for the part. I called him and he agreed to meet me outside my house at 10 p.m. My Resistingance plan was ready.

CHAPTER NINE

THE TOOTH FAIRY
AND TINY

The Plan involved getting Harry the Hulk to dress up as the tooth fairy.

Then he would tiptoe into Meg's room, wake her gently, tell her the curse was lifted and pop a few coins under her pillow.

Simple.

To really seal the deal, I decided that

Harry the Tooth Fairy would then bring Tiny into Meg's room to show her she was really fine and 'all was forgiven' or whatever she needed to hear.

After dinner, I snuck out to collect Tiny from Mr Hector's. It turns out that Tiny is hopeless at walking in a straight line so it took me a while to get her home.

This was made worse because I also bumped into Chas Cheeseman. I smelt him before I saw him.

He was wearing aftershave. Seriously! What kind of eleven-year-old wears aftershave?

Sadly, Tiny was attracted to the smell and rushed up to him. She started nuzzling him with her big piggy snout.

'Nice dog,' said Chas, half laughing, half sneering. 'What's its name?'

'Tiny,' I mumbled.

'Tiny! Funny name for such a huge fat pig.'

'She was meant to be tiny. She just isn't. She grew. A lot. That's all, really. Now I have to go, bye.'

Chas watched me trying to steer Tiny off down the pavement. Tiny kept weaving about and grunting. I could feel my cheeks burning.

'Looking forward to your party, by the way,' he shouted after me. 'I can't believe you're still not even eleven yet. I'm already thinking what to do when I turn twelve in a few weeks.'

Tiny swerved into a hedge. I followed her and sat there until I was sure he had gone.

When I finally turned the corner on to our street I could see Harry waiting outside. He had borrowed a pink ballet tutu from his sister, Kerry, and was wearing his mum's purple ski jacket and large sunglasses. He had also put on some pink lipstick, sprinkled glitter in his short black hair and draped a strand of silver tinsel round his neck.

The costume was so convincing that Tiny didn't recognise Harry. She sniffed him nervously. He took the tinsel off and said:

'It's me, Tiny, look!'

Tiny grunted approvingly and nuzzled in for a tickle.

I congratulated Harry on his look and we went inside. The house was silent. Everyone was in bed. It was quite late by now.

I left Tiny in the hallway and we tiptoed upstairs. Outside Meg's room I said:

'You go in, wake her up, tell her you're the tooth fairy and her curse is lifted. Then I'll bring in Tiny. OK?'

Harry was great as a fairy. Really convincing. But instead of looking pleased, Meg just looked terrified. Honestly!

As the tooth fairy was lifting the curse she just lay there, the duvet pulled up to her chin, shaking. I could see all this through the crack in the door.

Then it was my turn. I ran downstairs,

but where was Tiny? She wasn't in the hall any more.

I found her in the kitchen, face in the bin, scoffing potato peelings. I managed to lure her up the stairs with the last slice of Nana's vegan carob cake. I was at the top and she was halfway up when – disaster! The door to my parents' room opened.

Dad wandered out in his dressing gown, half asleep and heading for the bathroom. I dropped the cake and dived – literally dived – down the stairs. I heard the bathroom door shut. Phew! He hadn't spotted a thing.

But Tiny had already trotted up the stairs. When the bathroom door opened, Dad walked straight into her, screamed, jumped backwards and banged his head on the door frame. At this point, Harry appeared, dressed as a gigantic tooth fairy who likes skiing.

'Is he OK?' he asked, peering over Dad, who was flat out on the bathroom floor.

Dad began to mumble and open his eyes. Harry smiled at him. Some glitter from his hair floated down on to Dad's face.

'An angel!' said Dad. Then he touched his head. 'My headache has gone. It's a miracle!'

Harry had never been called an angel or a miracle before so he was pretty pleased, but there was no time to soak up the compliments. I didn't want to give Dad a chance to change his mind, so I rushed Harry out.

Then I checked on Meg. She was sitting next to Tiny on the floor. Now it was my turn for some acting.

'Whoa, crumbs, what is Tiny doing here?' I asked. I pretended to rub my eyes like I'd just woken up, too. It was a nice touch.

'The tooth fairy brought her,' said Meg.

'And did she lift your curse too?' I asked. 'Just, you know, possibly?'

'She *did*!' said Meg. 'How did you guess? That's exactly what she came to do. She said I didn't have to worry about my teeth falling out any more. She wasn't at all how I expected her to be – much taller – but oh, Tom, I'm so happy. Now I can eat biscuits again! And I can make you a birthday cake! Isn't that great?'

CHAPTER TEN

NANA NEXT

I slept in late, to recover from my amazing Resistingance plan. When I got up, the house felt different. The curtains were open. Meg was eating some noticeably crunchy toast at the kitchen table with no sign of mashing or Blu-Tack. This was good. This was brilliant, in fact! I could tick Meg off my family-fixing to-do list. My first victory!

Best of all, Meg was flicking through some of my books. I had a lot of books, mainly about volcanoes and gladiators, but I don't remember Meg asking to look at them.

'Don't panic, Tom. I won't spoil your precious books and I'll make sure they are correctly put back on the shelf in the exact alphabetical place, just how you like,' she said. 'I'm looking for inspiration.'

'Inspiration for what?' I asked.

'Your birthday cake,' she said. 'Mum and Dad might have cancelled your birthday, but I'll make sure you still have a cake.'

This was actually really nice of my little sister. Suddenly, someone in my family was on my side. It felt good. I didn't know what to say, so I ruffled her hair.

Then I noticed that the door to the dining-study was closed and the

DO NOT DISTURB, WRITER AT WORK

sign was up.

'Is Dad working?' I asked.

'Yes, he is,' said Nana. She was wearing a full-length paisley kaftan. A kaftan is like a giant dress. Nana loves a kaftan. 'He says he's had a vision. Your mother is hopeful this will be the inspiration he needs to finally finish his book.'

It seems my plan to fix Meg had also fixed Dad. **Result!** This was good. This was super good. With an angel vision to back Dad up, I reckoned he'd have his book done by tomorrow morning easily, if not before. My plan to fix my family was going beautifully. Meg and Dad were sorted already.

I checked the calendar. As I thought – two more days until my birthday. Then I noticed

Mum had written 'OVERTIME' across all those days, meaning she would be working extra hours then. I wanted to believe this was just a cover-up for 'TIME SPENT SHOPPING FOR COOL PRESENTS FOR TOM', but now I thought it probably was just overtime.

I ran up to Mum and Dad's room and checked the wardrobe or, as Meg and I like to call it, the 'pressie cupboard'. Mum always hides our Christmas and birthday presents in here. You can usually see packages and carrier bags stuffed in behind her dresses. Today, though, there were no packages.

It was clear to me now. Fixing Mum was **URGENT**.

If I was going to get my birthday un-cancelled, get some great presents and have an amazing day, Mum needed to work less.

But if Dad was about to finish his book, thanks to an angel-slash-tooth-fairy vision, that would change everything.

So I decided to skip past fixing Mum, the third thing on my list, and move straight to Nana.

I needed her to move back to her flat, so the house was ready for my Lucky Birthday. A Lucky Birthday that involved no dog ghosts, no kaftans, no vegan carob cake, no séances and definitely no saucers of Nosho Liver & Spleen lying around.

Back in the kitchen, Nana said she would like to go to the cafe with me; that it would cheer her up. I agreed. I wasn't sure if going to the cafe would help fix Nana, but her getting out and about was a start.

We walked down there, Nana moving surprisingly quickly for someone with a bruised hip.

'Found your pig yet?' Bruce asked.

I shushed him and pointed at Nana, who had gone to find a table.

'Murderer,' I whispered.

'Where?' said Bruce, grabbing a wooden spoon.

'No, the pig is a murderer,' I whispered. Then I mimed the pig falling off the roof and squashing Nana's dog. It was a really good mime, but Bruce looked confused.

Nana had sat down and hooked her bag over the chair next to her, but where was her walking stick? Hang on! She jumped up when the fire started the other day; she walked to the cafe without a stick …

'Your hip seems better,' I said.

'No, it's still quite sore,' said Nana, reading the menu.

'But you didn't use your walking stick when

you walked here and it's quite far, so I guess you'll be able to go back to your flat soon,' I said.

Nana dropped the menu and looked shocked. Ha, got you, you sly old granny, you! Then she sighed.

'All right, Tom,' she said. 'My hip does feel better.'

'I knew it!' I said. 'So why are you staying with us? Is it because you want to hear from Margherita?'

'I've given up on that, too, to be honest, since the séance nearly burned the house down,' said Nana. 'I accept that Margherita has gone. The truth is, Tom, I don't want to move back into my flat without her. It's lonely enough living without your grandad, but without my dog, too ...'

For a moment I thought she might cry. I held her hand. Poor Nana. I hadn't guessed she was lonely, and worried about living alone without even a small yappy dog for company. None of us had.

Persuading Nana to go back to her flat so I could have the house for my birthday party was on my to-do list, but that felt much more complicated now I understood why she was still living with us. How was I going to fix this? And with the countdown to my birthday ticking away like a mad unstoppable bomb?

Bruce came to take our order.

'Just a chai latte with soya milk please,' said Nana.

'Hmm,' said Bruce, chewing his pen. 'I can do you a tea.'

'You should broaden out your menu,' said Nana. 'Modernise it. Offer some vegetarian dishes.'

'Would they include bacon?' Bruce asked. 'Only I've got a job lot in the freezer.'

'How about some pasta dishes?' she said. 'Tom's dad makes incredible pasta sauces. Tom can bring you a jar if you like, to try it. Can't you, Tom?'

Oh, thanks, Nana – yet more for me to do! Didn't I have enough to be getting on with?

CHAPTER ELEVEN

A MAJOR TINY DISASTER

Back at the house, I thought about Nana not wanting to go home without her dog. I had to sort this out, for the sake of Nana and for the sake of my birthday, too. But what could I do? I couldn't bring Margherita back from the dead.

'Of course you can,' said Keith, over the

phone later. 'Just attach some jump leads and a battery. I've seen it done a thousand times.'

'Keith, are you nuts? My nana's chihuahua is as flat as an envelope and even less alive. She's in the freezer in a pizza box right now!'

'Perfect,' said Keith. 'You've kept the body fresh. Now just wire it back up and bingo! Dead dog problem solved.'

There is really no knowing what Keith will say sometimes, but I let it go and hung up.

Then I had a brilliant idea. I would find Nana a new dog. Yes – a cute puppy, to replace Margherita. I went online and found some chihuahua puppies for sale. Then I saw the price. Unbelievably, these tiny dogs with sticky-out eyes were £800 each! Someone pays £800 for a dog that looks like a strangled hamster. The world had gone mad.

Even so, I rang my mum to see if I could

borrow £800. She did a snorting noise down the phone, like an angry horse, and said she didn't have time to talk about this, as she was at work.

Then I rang Harry the Hulk to thank him for his work as the tooth fairy and asked him if he knew anyone who was giving away a dog. By a fantastic stroke of luck, he did.

'My Uncle Steve has a dog he doesn't want any more,' Harry said. 'I'll ask him if you can have it. Major's a nice dog. Very friendly.'

Harry was right – Major was very friendly. What Harry had not told me was that Major was also very big. He bounded into the living room and sat on Nana. It's possible Nana was trying to say something, but it was hard to tell – Major completely covered her. He was even bigger than Tiny!

Then Major licked Nana's face – his tongue

was the size of a towel – bounded off and galumphed around the living room, knocking things over. He found all the saucers of Nosho Liver & Spleen and wolfed the food down, too.

It was lucky that Meg was upstairs. She was even smaller than Nana, who had been nearly squashed by Major. I think Meg would have definitely been squashed by Major and I didn't want that. There had already been far too much squashing in this house as it was. Dad, though, was in his dining-study writing. He yelled at us to shut up.

I wanted to ask Nana if she liked Major and wanted to take him home, but she had shut herself in the kitchen, which was fortunate really because next thing we knew, Tiny came trotting down the stairs. Tiny! I had completely forgotten she was still in Meg's room.

Major was so excited to see a pig, he began

jumping around Tiny like an overgrown puppy. Our hallway is only the size of a sandwich and all of a sudden there was a pig, a gigantic jumping dog, a massively tall boy and me. Major and Tiny kept crashing into the kitchen door, causing Nana to shout 'Get away, get away!' until finally Dad screamed from inside his dining-study:

'Shut up, EVERYONE. I'm having my first creative breakthrough in months and I can't be interrupted by all this noise. I'm at the crucial final scene. It's essential I get this bit right!'

I managed to pin Tiny to the wall and stand between her and Major. Harry got Major on the lead and I shoved them both out of the front door and slammed it shut.

'That went well,' said Harry through the letter box. 'Such a friendly dog. I can't understand why my uncle wants to get rid of him.'

I found Nana hiding in the corner of the kitchen, just as she had after the séance fire. There was no point asking her if she wanted the dog. It was obviously not a match. I couldn't dwell on this though, I had to get Tiny back to Mr Hector's before Nana saw the pig that had murdered her chihuahua. I also had to drop a jar of Dad's pasta sauce down to Bruce at the cafe.

I grabbed the sauce, grabbed the pig and left.

CHAPTER TWELVE

I FEEL LIKE CHICKEN TONIGHT

It took me ages to make it to the cafe. Tiny still hadn't learned how to walk in a straight line. It was OK, though, as this gave me more time to think about how to find a replacement for Nana's dead dog.

With Meg free from her curse and Dad really nearly finishing his book again, I was inching closer to getting my birthday uncancelled. If I could find a replacement for Margherita so that Nana was happy to go home, I was almost there.

My thinking was interrupted by that smell again; a smell that was painful to my nose. The smell of Chas Cheeseman and his expensive aftershave. He was just leaving the park, riding an incredibly smart, shiny bike. He stopped.

'Look who it is,' he said. 'It's Tom out for a walk with his pig-dog. What's its name again? Mini? Titchy?'

'Tiny,' I said.

'Tiny, of course,' he said. 'Do you like my new bike? Early birthday present. Twelve gears because I'm twelve. Cool, isn't it? What are you getting for your birthday? When is it again?'

Luckily, Tiny had caught the whiff of a half-eaten Kit Kat in the bushes and was off, so I said goodbye and ran after her.

Eventually, I managed to steer Tiny out of the bushes, and at the cafe I handed Bruce the jar of Dad's pasta sauce.

'Could I add a bit of bacon to this, do you think?' Bruce asked.

'Please don't say "bacon" in front of my pig,' I said, indicating Tiny.

'Sorry! Didn't see it there,' said Bruce. 'You found it then?'

'Yes,' I said.

'What's in it?' said Bruce.

'The pig?'

'No, the sauce.'

'Oh sorry, I don't know,' I said. 'It's Dad's top-secret recipe.'

'I'll just put *Pasta with Mystery Sauce* on the menu,' said Bruce.

Tiny started grunting happily when we went through the gate to Mr Hector's place. The chickens all clustered round me again, but I didn't have time for any whispering. I was still too busy puzzling over what to do about Nana.

I asked Mr Hector how I could find a

replacement for Nana's dead dog. I explained how Major was too big and how chihuahuas cost billions of pounds that I didn't have. The chickens were staring at me the whole time, like I was the most amazing person they'd ever seen.

'Sometimes the answer's right in front of your nose,' said Mr Hector, smiling.

Then my phone rang.

It was Keith.

'I was just wondering how the bank job went last night,' he said. 'Are you rich now?'

'There was no bank job, Keith!' I yelled.

'That's a shame,' he said. 'I was hoping to borrow a fiver.'

Keith's completely pointless phone call made me feel flustered. Was everything pointless? My birthday was only two days away. The hours seemed to be disappearing fast, like tiny mice running into the fog, and I still hadn't fixed Nana or Mum. Could I do it? Should I just give up?

Feeling panicked, I ran home.

Dad was still writing – good.

Meg wasn't trying to stick her teeth in place with Blu-Tack – also good.

Nana was having a cup of tea and not consulting crystals or doing a Mystic Morris – definitely good, too.

I still had not found her a replacement dog, though – not good.

I sat at the table, thinking hard. Then I felt a tickling sensation on my cheek. It was a chicken feather stuck in my collar. I plucked it out and stared at it hard, which is not as hard as thinking hard, but still requires concentration. And then I could hear

Mr Hector saying, 'Sometimes the answer's right in front of your nose.'

Yes!

I legged it back to Mr Hector's and found him still sitting under the apple tree, his pipe in his mouth. The chickens immediately lined up behind me as I asked him:

'Can I have a chicken?'

'For your nana?' he said.

'For my nana, that's right. Hang on! How did you know?'

Mr Hector just laughed.

'Of course. Poultry make great pets.'

'Great. How should I choose one?' I asked.

'You're the chicken whisperer. You work it out.'

Oh yes, I was the chicken whisperer. That.

I looked at the chickens. I counted ten in

total. They were all lined up in front of me, silent, looking up at me.

'Chickens!' I said. I was trying to sound cool and in charge. I spread my arms wide. 'Which one of you will come with me on a mission both serious and important? A big mission, to save my birthday and also cheer up an old lady in a kaftan.'

Solemnly, each chicken raised its right wing.

'No, I only need one,' I said. 'Didn't you hear me? Sorry. Only one chicken.'

The chickens gathered in a little circle like they were having a chat, then one chicken stepped forward. She was the smallest of all the chickens, but she had nice brown feathers and a twinkle in her eye.

'Good,' I said. 'You are the chosen one. Come forth, Chosen One.'

The chicken hopped on to my arm and perched there, like a hawk or an eagle. I stroked its soft feathers.

'Shall we go?'

The chicken nodded.

CHAPTER THIRTEEN

LET DOWN AND HANGING AROUND

Nana was pretty surprised when I walked in.

'You can't bring a chicken into the house,' she spluttered.

'This is no ordinary chicken!' I said. I demonstrated to Nana that I had complete control over the chicken – I am the chicken whisperer, after all – by getting it to do a couple of backflips, and then Nana relaxed.

The chicken sat on her lap. Nana stroked its feathers. The chicken clucked quietly. It was actually a very touching scene.

'Oh, Tom,' said Nana, looking at me with tears in her eyes. 'She's lovely.'

'I thought you'd like another pet, Nana,' I explained.

'You did all this for me?' Nana said. 'That's so kind. I shall name her Caesar.'

'As in chicken Caesar salad?' I said. Another pet named after a food item. Margherita pizza and now chicken Caesar. This might not end well …

'No, because once you sees her, you loves her,' said Nana, laughing.

It was a terrible joke and a rubbish name, but this was the first time Nana had laughed since Margherita died, so I let it go.

Meg came in holding a recipe book.

'I can't decide which kind of cake to make you, Tom,' she said.

Then she whispered: 'I meant what I said earlier. Even if Mum and Dad still cancel your birthday, we can still eat it.'

I had to admit that was nice, although I really didn't want to think about the possibility of my birthday staying cancelled. Things were going well. Really well. Resistingance had worked. It felt good.

I shut my eyes and imagined Dad coming out of his dining-study any minute, triumphant, waving a thick wad of papers and shouting that he'd finally finished his book, saying that seeing an angel had inspired him and the book was done and brilliant and would sell millions of copies!

Then I pictured Mum walking in from

work, hearing the news that Dad had finished his book, and them hugging and dancing round the kitchen. Best of all, I could see them all turning to me, beaming, and saying, 'Tom, your birthday is back on, and we're going to make it better than ever. The best, most amazing Lucky Birthday in the world!' Then Nana would set off for her own flat, her chicken on her arm, Meg by her side. And Meg would turn to me and say, 'You have my room, Tom, you deserve it.' Yes!

BING BONG!

The doorbell woke me from my very nice daydream. It was Harry the Hulk. He thought perhaps he'd left Major's ball round here earlier and could he look for it? I let him in.

I wish I hadn't.

Meg stared at Harry as he searched around for the ball. She peered at his head while he crawled along the floor, looking under the sofa. And then she shrieked.

'Glitter! In your hair!' She pressed her hand to her mouth. 'You're the tooth fairy!'

Harry stood up straight. He looked nervously at me.

'You're the angel!' said Dad, pointing his pen at Harry. I hadn't even heard Dad come out of his dining-study.

'I can explain,' I blurted. But no one was listening. Meg, still clutching her mouth, raced upstairs to her room. Dad dropped his pen.

'I wasn't visited by an angel sent on a divine mission to inspire me,' said Dad. 'It was just a kid with glitter and tinsel on!'

'But why does it matter if it's helping you write?' I asked.

'It matters because it was a lie,' said Dad.

'I thought I had divine powers on my side, that someone was helping me.'

'What's this?' asked Mum, back from work.

'The angel vision was just Tom's friend wearing glitter,' said Dad. 'My creative streak was based on a lie. It's over.'

Then Mum started shouting, saying Dad was never going to finish his book, was he? And he said it wasn't his fault, and there was lots of other shouting. Then Nana appeared with her bags packed and asked for a lift home.

Mum and Dad stopped and both pointed at chicken Caesar, standing next to her.

'What's that?' they asked at the same time.

'It's Caesar, my new pet, which Tom kindly got for me so I won't be lonely. I'm ready to go home now.'

But as Nana moved towards the front door, the chicken stopped following her and hopped on to my arm instead.

'Go with Nana,' I said. But the chicken wouldn't budge. I suppose, as I was the chicken whisperer, the chicken wanted to stay with me. All I knew for sure was that this wasn't part of the plan. Neither was Mum grabbing her car keys and leading Nana towards the front door.

'Don't worry, Mum, you won't be lonely,' she said. 'I'm coming with you. I'm moving out.'

'Jill, come on!' said Dad, but Mum followed Nana outside and slammed the front door behind her.

Dad stomped back into his dining-study and slammed the door.

Meg, who had been watching from the top of the stairs, went back into her room and slammed *her* door.

Harry slunk off to the kitchen and slammed that door (although I think that was an accident).

I was left in the hallway again. I wasn't sitting in a saucer of Nosho Liver & Spleen this time, but it felt exactly the same. The same feeling of doom and failure and misery. My plan to fix my family was in pieces. My birthday was still cancelled.

CHAPTER FOURTEEN

BY ME, FOR ME

I expected to find Meg stuffing Blu-Tack round her teeth again when I went into her room. In fact, she was just sitting on her bed. She threw a book at me.

'That's for sending a fake tooth fairy,' she said.

'I only wanted you to stop worrying that everything was your fault,' I said.

'Yeah, so I could go to Nana's and you could use my room, I bet.'

How had she guessed that? It's like she'd read my mind. I often forgot how smart Meg was. She liked things like ponies and dancing and hairgrips, but alongside all that was some weird nine-year-old smartness.

'It's OK, Tom,' she said, patting the bed next to her. I sat down.

'I will still make your cake, but I want to be in on the party *and* the sleepover.'

'Well, at this rate, there isn't going to be either,' I said. 'It's still cancelled, and now Mum's moved out and Dad's stopped writing. I need to face it – my birthday is over. Mum hasn't even bought any presents.'

'Did you check the pressie cupboard?' Meg asked.

I nodded.

'Did you check right to the back?' she asked.

'Right to the back,' I said. 'So far back I found Mum's old gardening trousers, from when she used to have an allotment, before she started working so much. Not a single present though.'

We were both silent.

'I'm sure Dad hasn't planned any ace snacks for me, and I don't think either of them has organised an outing or treat. It's off, over, not happening. I thought I could fix everyone and my birthday would be back on, but I was wrong. My parents have really, truly cancelled my birthday.'

'Do you think Mum will come home?' Meg asked.

'I don't know.'

'Do you think Dad will finish his book?' Meg asked.

'I don't know.'

'This is serious,' said Meg.

'I know,' I said.

'This was your Lucky Birthday, too,' said Meg.

'I know.'

We sat quietly for a minute. Meg held my hand, which was weird, but I found that I quite liked it.

Then Harry put his head around the door. I'd completely forgotten he was here.

'Found Major's ball,' he said. 'I'll be off then. See you on your birthday.'

'It's cancelled,' I said. 'Tell everyone – Keith, Jonny, Chas, everyone.'

'Oh, right,' said Harry, and then he left.

'Bye, tooth fairy,' Meg shouted after him.

We sat quietly for a while. Chicken Caesar had tiptoed in at some point and was now sitting between us. Then my phone rang. It was Keith again.

'I've just seen Harry and he said your birthday is cancelled,' he said. 'Is that true?'

'I told you about this, Keith, remember? Then I tried to do Resistingance and fight back but it hasn't worked,' I explained. 'It's still cancelled.'

'Did you try the other one?' he said. 'Resilience.'

'That just means putting up with stuff and being strong, doesn't it?' I said.

'To be honest, I've never been quite sure what it means,' Keith said. 'If I were you I'd just do it myself.'

'Do what myself?'

'Do your birthday yourself,' Keith said. 'Remember when I waited ages for my mum to sort out a hair appointment for me and she never did? I just cut my hair myself.'

'Yeah, but that didn't work out too well, Keith,' I said. 'You looked like you'd been attacked by pelicans.'

'And remember when my dad was going to get me a dentist appointment and he never did?' Keith went on. 'I just made a brace myself, from an old coat hanger and some elastic bands.'

'That also didn't work out too well,' I said. 'You couldn't eat or close your mouth.'

'The point is,' Keith said, 'sometimes grown-ups don't do what they should for their kids because they're busy, or whatever the excuse is, and so us kids just have to do it ourselves.'

I thought about this for a second. Then I found myself saying words I never thought I'd say.

'Keith, you are a genius! An absolute genius!'

'Correct,' said Keith.

'I'll organise my birthday myself. I've already done the invites. Meg can make the cake. Of course! Best of all, I don't have to wait to see what Mum and Dad do. I can design it all myself – every last detail, every last moment, exactly as I want it. My parents might have cancelled my birthday, but I haven't.

And I say – it's back on, on, ON,

ON!'

CHAPTER FIFTEEN

A MAN IN PANTS

I grabbed a notebook and wrote **MY BIRTHDAY** at the top. I thought hard.

I had never planned a birthday for myself. It was exciting, but also a bit scary. Where to begin?

'Chas Cheeseman's party had fireworks and a chef and people brought huge presents and ...'

'Who cares what Chas Cheeseman had,' Meg said. 'What do *you* want?'

I thought hard and then made a few notes:

1. Must be awesome, fun, exciting and something everyone remembers for ages – LUCKY BIRTHDAY!

2. Food – ask Bruce in cafe for help?

3. Party here or somewhere else?

4. Open presents *first*!

Then my stomach rumbled. I was starving. It had been a busy day. I hadn't had dinner.

Dad had not come out of his dining-study. The house was strangely quiet. Meg and I opened a jar of Dad's top-secret-recipe pasta sauce and had it with some cold leftover spaghetti we found in the fridge. I had forgotten how delicious his sauce was. Even when served with cold spaghetti.

Mum called to say goodnight and tell us she would be back tomorrow. She said Nana seemed happy to be home, even without chicken Caesar. I told chicken Caesar she was off the hook.

I lay in bed with my notebook, making more birthday plans.

Next thing I knew, it was morning.

I could only explain this time travel in one way – I had fallen asleep.

This also meant that it was no longer Thursday, it was Friday.

My birthday was Saturday. Tomorrow!

Not a second to lose.

I ran to the cafe to ask Bruce if he could supply some food for my birthday party. He suggested bacon sandwiches. I agreed.

'You can pay me in your dad's pasta sauce,' he said. 'It's selling really well here. People love it. They love it more than my bacon sandwiches.'

Party food – sorted! And all before 9.30 a.m. Yes!

'Is that yours?' Bruce said, pointing across the cafe.

Chicken Caesar was standing on one of the tables, pecking up crumbs. She must have followed me here. I whistled and she hopped up on my arm.

'Wow!' said Bruce. 'What are you, some kind of chicken whisperer or something, with weird powers over chickens?'

There was no time to explain. I just winked and left.

When I got back to the house, I could hear the sound of laughter and running around.

Mum? Dad? My heart skipped a beat for a second. But it was just Meg and Keith. Meg and Keith had always got along. Keith's actual sister was older and super brainy. Keith said Meg was way more fun.

Meg was riding around the living room on Keith's back – she had always wanted a pony – and Keith was screaming 'Help me, help me!' for some reason.

They were laughing a lot. This was typical. No sense of urgency. They might have time for messing about, but I didn't. I had my birthday to save.

'Stop, both of you!' I commanded. 'Keith, why are you here and what do you want?'

'I've come to help plan your birthday,' Keith said. 'You said I was a **genius**. Which is true. So, I'm here to offer my genius skills.'

I now regretted calling Keith a genius. Would he ever stop reminding me of that? But maybe some help would be good. With only one day to go, time was running out and there was still a lot to arrange.

'In that case, stop pretending to be a pony and get upstairs now,' I said.

'He's not a pony,' said Meg. 'We're re-enacting that time you got pounced on by a lamb when we all went to the farm. Keith is you and I'm the lamb, squashing you.'

Keith shouted 'Help me, help me, get it off me!' a few more times, and the pair of them collapsed on to the floor laughing. I had thought Meg was smart and Keith a genius, but I was now changing my mind.

'I didn't say help me,' I said quickly. 'I fought the lamb off, you're remembering it all wrong. Anyway, shut up about the lamb attack. There is no time for this. Please! We have a birthday to save.'

We ran upstairs to my room. Dad appeared on the landing. He had only just got up, even though it was 10 a.m.! He looked extremely scruffy. Worst of all, he was in his pants. Only his pants.

This was very disturbing and could possibly ruin all my birthday plans. How could I have a birthday at home if Dad was going to wander in wearing only his pants? What if Chas Cheeseman saw that? I didn't remember every last detail of Chas's amazing party, but I'm pretty certain that at no point did his dad walk in wearing only his pants.

I couldn't worry about it now, there was just way too much else to sort out. I handed Keith and Meg a pen and paper.

'I need suggestions for my birthday,' I said. 'Things to do, activities ...'

'Things to do and activities are the same thing,' said Meg.

I gave her a strong look.

Meg began making notes. Keith was looking at my bookshelf for ideas.

'You've got a lot of books about volcanoes,' he said. Then he found one about gladiators.

'Tom J. Bostock?' he said, noticing my name inside the front jacket. 'What's the J stand for?'

'It's my middle name,' I said.

'Mum and Dad didn't give us middle names,' said Meg.

'I gave myself one,' I said.

'What is it then?' Keith asked.

'Jemath,' I said.

'Jemath?!' Keith said.

'I made it up. It's a cool name,' I said.

Meg started laughing. I gave her another strong look. Keith was smirking. I gave him a strong look, too.

'Get on with it!' I said. 'Ideas, now! No time to lose!'

'OK, whatever you say, Tom Jemath Bostock,' Keith muttered. Meg giggled some more. I gave them both strong looks.

A few moments later we were interrupted by Dad shouting and banging about in the bathroom. Chicken Caesar had snuck into the shower with him. Dad shooed her out and I made her sit at the end of the bed, still wet. I had to give her a strong look, too. Honestly!

'What ideas have you got?' I asked. 'I don't have much time, so let's have a look.'

They passed me their lists.

Keith's list looked like this:

fireworks and/or fire

helicopter flight

reptiles

jet packs for all guests

fudge

Meg's list looked like this:

horse riding

kittens

magic

bunting

'Where am I going to get jet packs from, Keith?' I asked.

'Internet?' he said.

'And how am I going to pay for them?' I said. 'If a chihuahua puppy costs £800, I dread to think what a jet pack costs. At least that, probably. I don't have £800.'

'How much money do you have?' Meg asked.

I checked my wallet. £8.62.

'That rules out a helicopter flight and fireworks, too,' I said, crossing them off Keith's list.

'And horse riding,' I added, crossing that off Meg's list.

'I still think there are some good ideas here,' said Meg. 'Do you have any better ones?'

I checked my own list. 'I've got here: must be awesome, fun, exciting and something everyone remembers for ages.'

'Which is what?' said Meg.

The sound of Dad shouting downstairs boomed up to us before I could answer.

We found him in the kitchen, still in his pants. This was disturbing (again).

Even more disturbing – he was jabbing at chicken Caesar with a wooden spoon and defending himself with a pan lid, as she tried to grab cold spaghetti from a plate on the table and peck him at the same time.

'Get off!' he yelled. 'I'll make kebabs out of you!'

This was no way to talk to a chicken.

'She probably thinks the spaghetti is worms,' I explained.

'It's not worms, it's my breakfast!' said Dad.

I didn't comment on the utter rubbishness of this breakfast. Dad was supposed to be an amazing cook. How could he settle for cold spaghetti at 10.30 in the morning? And what was he doing getting up so late? It was all very sloppy.

But never mind. No time to worry about this. I suddenly remembered Mr Hector saying, 'Sometimes the answer is right in front of your nose.'

I thought of the volcano and gladiator books in my room. And then I looked at the scene in front of me.

The answer really was in front of my nose, in the form of a hungry chicken and a middle-aged man in pants.

CHAPTER SIXTEEN

PLANS, PLACES AND DIY PROPS

The sight of Dad with a wooden-spoon sword and pan-lid shield made an impression on me (and it wasn't just the fact that he was only wearing pants at the time). He looked like a warrior; like a fighter; like a gladiator!

I thought of my gladiator book that Keith had flicked through and all the pictures of warriors fighting wild animals in the Colosseum of ancient Rome, while the crowds roared. That was it! Gladiatorial combat. The perfect birthday entertainment! Some kids get taken to the cinema for their birthday, but I would create my own epic show, with gladiators, wild beasts and plenty of drama. That would be awesome, fun, exciting and something everyone would remember for ages.

Plus, it wouldn't cost much, which was good, as I only had £8.62.

I dropped chicken Caesar at Mr Hector's and quickly explained that the poultry-as-pet plan hadn't worked.

'Your nana can always come and visit the chickens here if she's lonely,' Mr Hector suggested.

'But what about Tiny?' I said. 'Tiny killed

her chihuahua. I'm not sure Nana could cope with seeing Tiny again.'

Mr Hector chewed his pipe a bit. 'Not a problem,' he said. 'I can disguise her.'

'What as?'

'A pony ...' he said. 'Done it loads of times back in my village, when I was a young 'un. Dress a pig up as a pony, you can steal it right out from under the farmer's nose.'

This got me thinking.

'Do you do zebras?' I asked Mr Hector. 'I mean, could you disguise Tiny as a zebra?'

Mr Hector chewed his pipe a bit more and then agreed to give it a go. The chickens looked excited.

'What you got planned, then, that you need a pig-zebra for?' he asked.

I explained about my DIY birthday extravaganza show. He liked the sound of it.

Then I asked if I could have my birthday in his garden, on the grass right here, under the apple tree.

'It's the perfect space; so much better than my house,' I said. 'Plus, I can't risk my friends seeing my dad in his pants.'

Mr Hector agreed – about the show and the pants. He said he'd make some birthday preparations. The chickens looked *really* excited now.

I probably looked really excited, too. I definitely felt really excited. My birthday plans were taking shape:

Food – yes.
Venue – yes.
Things to do and activities – yes.

I would have an awesome Lucky Birthday after all!

Meg and Keith were in the kitchen when I got home.

Keith was reading one of my volcano books. This gave me another idea. Not only would there be gladiatorial combat, it would be set in the shadow of the mighty volcano Vesuvius! This would make my birthday show extra exciting.

I wasn't sure if there were gladiators at the same time as Vesuvius but I didn't care. It was my party and I could have gladiators and Vesuvius erupting if I wanted to.

'Meg,' I said, 'can you make a volcano cake?'

She looked at the pictures of Vesuvius and nodded slowly, thinking.

'Yeah, I can make you a volcano cake,' she said. 'Chocolate sponge, greyish icing, strawberry laces for lava. I can make this work.'

151

'Brilliant!' I said.

My heart was thumping now. I held my hands up in the air, clasped together. I was panting a little. I could picture my birthday show clearly. I could see it! I could almost touch it ... And it was beautiful!

The gladiators would fight with wild beasts and then – oh no! – Vesuvius would erupt, sending rocks and hot ash raining down on the Colosseum, with strawberry-laces lava pouring out, forcing the fighters and the animals to flee in terror. (I didn't quite know yet how I'd pull off the rocks and hot ash, but I'd work something out.) And the result would be awesome, awesome, **AWESOME!**

Forget Chas Cheeseman and his fireworks and private chef, this birthday was the one that would go down in history!

'Are you all right, Tom?' Keith asked. 'You look like you've seen a unicorn.'

'I've figured out my birthday,' I said, grinning. 'I've done it! I'm going to put on a birthday show. You're all going to be in it. It's going to be amazing. Don't ask questions now, I don't have time, just tell me, where can I get props?'

Keith scratched his head.

'A DIY store?' he said. 'This is a do-it-yourself birthday, so you should probably go to a do-it-yourself store.'

'Genius!' I said. It just slipped out. This was the second time in two days I'd called Keith a genius. I had to stop this. It was going to Keith's head.

As we walked to the nearby DIY store I explained the concept of the show to Keith. He nodded.

'That sounds pretty cool,' he said.

Too right it did.

The store was a huge place, full of planks and radiators and entire kitchens and bags of screws.

Keith got trapped behind a forklift truck in the laminate-flooring aisle for a while, but eventually, we found all kinds of essential items – gold spray paint, a piece of netting, some thick string, a long plastic pipe, some plastic plant pots.

It came to £8.39, which gave me 17p change … No hang on, about 20p change … Never mind. The point is, I could afford it.

Back at home, we got to work.

Keith cut a piece out of each plant pot so they were shaped like helmets and I spray-painted them gold.

I also spray-painted the wheelbarrow and

wrote **CHARIOT** down the side in marker pen, just for clarity. We broke the pipe up into spear and sword lengths and gathered up a few things from the house, too:

Some flour from Meg's baking session.
Some saucepan lids.

We piled the props in the wheelbarrow, ready for my birthday the next day.

I shook Keith's hand. He said something about 'strength and honour', then went home for his lunch.

CHAPTER SEVENTEEN

THANK GOODNESS
FOR ME

With the props sorted for my epic gladiator volcano birthday show, the next thing I had to think about was costumes.

Harry the Hulk had done such a good job of his tooth-fairy costume that I decided he was the best person to help with this. I raided Meg's dressing-up box and then ran over to

Harry's house to drop off what I'd found and brief him on the show.

As I left, Major bounded in from the garden and knocked me over.

'Sorry,' said Harry. 'My uncle doesn't want him back so we're looking after him for now. He's so friendly, but he's also the size of a horse and twice as strong.'

This gave me an idea, which I quickly discussed with Harry. I popped in at Bruce's cafe on my way home, to check he knew what time to deliver the birthday sandwiches. I had to squeeze past a queue of people waiting to go in.

'They all want to have pasta with your dad's mystery sauce on,' said Bruce. 'It's a sensation. I had the local paper here yesterday. Everyone's talking about it and taking photos, which they put on the so-so media – Instant Gran, or something. They never did that with my bacon sarnies.'

It was late afternoon by the time I got home. The house smelt of birthday cake, but Meg wouldn't let me see it.

Nana had popped round and was sitting at the kitchen table, reading a book about poultry management. She wanted to see chicken Caesar. I explained that she was living not far from here, safe and happy, in a lovely secret garden.

'If I see her again, I'm sure I can win her over so she'll come and live with me,' said Nana. 'Can we go and visit her now? Or go first thing tomorrow?'

'Tomorrow is my birthday, Nana! Have you forgotten as well? What is wrong with all the adults in this family?'

I shouted.

I didn't mean to shout. It just burst out of me. Just because Mum and Dad had cancelled

my birthday, did that mean my own nana
had to completely forget, too?

Nana looked shocked, probably because I'd
shouted at her, but maybe also because she'd
clean forgotten about my birthday and was
shocked at how un-Nana-ish that was.

'I'm sorry. I promise I'll take you to see
chicken Caesar,' I said, 'but tomorrow I have

birthday things to do with my friends. We can go the day after.'

I spent a few hours writing the script for tomorrow's gladiator-volcano spectacular up in my room, and then rang Keith and Harry to let them know we were meeting outside my house at 7 a.m. sharp. I always wake up early on my birthday, after all.

A little later, Mum came home. She ruffled my hair. She said she was really sorry for cancelling my birthday and promised we would do it all later.

I felt like doing the fingers-in-the-air thing around the word **'later'**. What did 'later' even mean? The next day? Three weeks' time? Never, more like!

Mum also said she had to work tomorrow, even though it was a Saturday. I didn't say anything, but I could feel my cheeks going hot.

I was imagining the birthday I might have had, the cancelled one, and it wasn't pretty. Me sitting in my room all day, my mum at work, my dad sulking and not writing his book, and my nana going on about visiting a chicken. There would be Meg's cake, but that would be it. Thank goodness for Meg. She understood how important this birthday was to me. She was the only person in my family who did.

Then I thought about my epic gladiator-volcano plan and about the fun I'd have with my friends tomorrow and felt better. I might not get many presents, my mum and dad wouldn't even be there (not invited) but I was determined it would be a day that was awesome, fun, exciting and a party that everyone remembered for ages.

And it was. All those things. And more. **Much more**.

CHAPTER EIGHTEEN

HAPPY BIRTHDAY!

I woke up at 6.30 a.m. Saturday, 11th August. Happy birthday to me! I was outside the house with the wheelbarrow-slash-chariot full of essential props by 7 a.m. sharp. Sadly, no one else was.

I had to go back inside and wake up Meg. And I had to remind her to bring my cake. Honestly!

At 7.30 a.m., Keith wandered up the road, yawning. I gave him a strong look. Then I had to remind him to say happy birthday.

Honestly again!

Then Major the dog jumped on Keith from behind and knocked him into a hedge. This at least woke Keith up properly.

'Sorry, Major seems extra excited this morning,' said Harry the Hulk.

Major was trying to leap at my birthday cake, which Meg had concealed in a large cardboard box.

'We have to keep Major away from that cake, Harry,' I said. 'It's an essential prop and foodstuff for today.'

'Is Jonny coming?' Keith asked.

'Yes,' I said. Then I remembered. Harry had let everyone know that my birthday was cancelled and I had forgotten to tell him it was back on. **Curses!**

'We'll call round for him,' I said. 'Then I will brief you all on how the gladiator-volcano show will go. Harry, you carry the cake. You're the only one tall enough to keep it out of the way of Major.'

We set off, wearing our golden plant pot helmets. Major led the way, with me and Keith being dragged along behind him. Harry the Hulk was carrying my cake in its box on his head, which left Meg to push the wheelbarrow-slash-chariot at the rear.

We were in good spirits, and must have looked impressive, our golden helmets gleaming in the morning sun, Major surging out in front like a powerful charger. Several cars peeped at us as they passed, the drivers waving, pointing and laughing.

Before we reached Jonny's place, we had to pass Chas Cheeseman's posh house.

Sadly, this did not go well.

I blame Chas's cats. They were sitting in the front garden.

Why couldn't they have been sitting in the back garden? Or indoors? Anyway, just the sight of them sent Major crazy.

He yanked so hard he pulled me and Keith off our feet. We lost control of him and he chased after the cats, all across Chas

Cheeseman's very posh front garden.

Major crashed through the flower beds, splashed through the pond and knocked over a statue of a woman wearing a curtain. Luckily, it had one arm missing so was clearly already damaged.

Then he chased the cats up a tree and barked loudly at them. Mr Cheeseman then shouted out of the window at us.

We had all forgotten to tell Chas that the party was back on, but we were too busy getting Major under control to do that now

and, honestly, I realised I didn't really care if he was there or not, with his fancy bike and his smelly aftershave. I had my real friends, and I was going to have my very own homemade birthday, too.

I did really want Jonny to come, though. By the time we made it round to his, we were a bit stressed, and Harry the Hulk had already lost his golden plant pot helmet.

We knocked on the door a few times and finally Jonny's brother Ted answered. He burst out laughing when he saw us.

'Nice pipes,' he said, pointing at our spears. 'And what have you done to that wheelbarrow?'

'It's a chariot,' I explained. 'Is your brother here? It's my birthday today and I've un-cancelled it. We're putting on a gladiator show and having bacon sarnies and cake. He's invited.'

'Sorry, Jonny hates birthdays and cake and all that other stuff and doesn't want to come,' said Ted, but Jonny elbowed him out of the way and stood grinning in the doorway. He was still wearing his pyjamas. Major licked his toes.

'Ignore my brother, he's an idiot,' Jonny said. 'Wow, you guys look amazing! Love the hats.'

'Helmets!' I said.

'What are we doing?' Jonny asked.

'I'll explain when we get there,' I said. 'Let's go. You can stay in your PJs – we have costumes.'

We set off again. Jonny wished me happy birthday. Major calmed down a bit, obviously exhausted from his cat rampage in Chas Cheeseman's front garden, and soon we reached Mr Hector's secret garden.

He had decorated the front gate with

bunting. Greyish-white bunting.

'I think it's made of old pants,' whispered Meg.

The chickens were waiting for us just inside the gate. They clucked and flapped and hopped on and off our heads, obviously incredibly excited about my birthday – quite right, too.

I got them to do a couple of backflips.

Everyone clapped.

Then we walked into Mr Hector's garden – a few chickens riding on Major's back – through the thick bushes and up the shady path to the grassy area that would become our Colosseum.

Mr Hector was sitting under his apple tree (which also had pants bunting in it) but, hang on, sitting alongside him was …

'Nana!' I shouted, dropping a chicken. 'What are you doing here?'

CHAPTER NINETEEN
GAMES ON ...

I had not expected to find Nana at my birthday celebrations, but it was very nice to see her.

She hugged me, wished me happy birthday and gave me a present wrapped in purple tissue paper. It was a kaftan. She slipped it over my golden plant pot helmet.

'They're extremely comfortable,' she said.

Jonny sniggered.

I reminded him that he was still in his pyjamas, which were decorated with space rockets.

He shut up.

Nana explained that last night, she had gone out looking for the garden where chicken Caesar might be, had heard clucking and seen Mr Hector at the gate, putting up his pants bunting. They got talking and realised they both knew me. Then Mr Hector explained all about my birthday show taking place here and invited Nana along.

'He's a very lovely man,' Nana added. Mr Hector smiled at her. She smiled at him.

'What about Tiny?' I whispered to Mr Hector. 'Did she see the pig? The pig that killed her chihuahua? She would freak out if she did.'

Mr Hector patted his nose with one finger.

'All fully disguised,' he said, and winked. 'She's in the kitchen.'

We tied Major to the apple tree, unloaded the wheelbarrow-slash-chariot and used the twine to mark out a ring on the grass.

'This is the Colosseum,' I said. 'Nana and Mr Hector, you can be spectators. Harry and Jonny, you are gladiators and need to fight the wild animals in the Colosseum. Keith is narrator and on special effects and I'm the Roman emperor.'

'What about me?' asked Meg. 'I want to be a gladiator. Girls can be gladiators too.'

'She's right,' said Keith. 'I saw a TV programme about it once.'

I agreed Meg could come on in the beginning as a gladiator, so long as she was ready to unbox the volcano cake at the right moment.

I decided that Nana's kaftan would be excellent for a Roman emperor's robes. I just added a belt made of twine and swapped my golden plant pot helmet for some ivy, which was growing up Mr Hector's apple tree.

Jonny, Harry and Meg dressed in the cardboard armour that Harry had made, then Harry put the pink tutu on that he'd worn when he was the tooth fairy. I pointed out

that this was not historically accurate. He said he wanted 'to put the glad back into gladiator'. I let it go.

Then I briefed the chickens on their role – they had to pretend to attack the gladiators, as if they were wild animals fighting for their life – but only when I said they could.

Then I went to find Tiny. I peeped through the kitchen window. She was asleep on the floor. It wasn't until I opened the door and the daylight poured in that I saw ... Tiny, but not Tiny. A pig ... but also a zebra.

'Wow!'

Mr Hector had done a superb job. Tiny was covered in black-and-white stripes. He had even fixed a mane and tail to Tiny, made out of straw. This was fantastic. Tiny would really give the show extra awesomeness, plus Nana would never recognise her or realise that this zebra was in fact the pig that killed her dog.

Back at the Colosseum, everyone was lined up – even the chickens.

'You look great. Thank you to everyone for coming today, and for sharing my birthday. And now, let the games—'

'Hang on,' said Meg. 'We've got something for you. A present.'

Presents!

I had completely forgotten about presents. I had written on my list of birthday activities 'Open presents *first*!', but since designing the show and organising everything, I'd forgotten all about presents. They didn't seem that important any more (weird, I know).

Meg handed me a book. A scrapbook, filled with messages and photos and recipes and drawings and poems – and everyone had added something to it. There was even a paw print and some hairs from Major.

I flicked through.

Harry had done an amazing sketch of himself as the tooth fairy. Jonny had written a rude rhyme. There were photos of me and Keith aged four, with ice cream round our faces. Meg had drawn a sketch of the volcano cake. There was a photo of Meg just before I pushed her into a stream on holiday. A photo of Tiny when she was actually tiny and before she had to live on the roof. Photos of Mum and Dad, smiling, back when they used to smile …

'It's lovely,' I said, feeling a bit strange.

'What do you say?' Keith said.

'Thank you,' I said.

'No, you nerd, we don't care about that. You say – let the games commence!'

'Oh right, yes!'

I ran to the side of the Colosseum. Meg, Jonny and Harry the Hulk raised their plastic pipe swords and spears and picked up their pan-lid shields. The chickens tensed up again, waiting for the signal. I spread my arms wide, counted one, two, three – and shouted:

'Let the games commence!'

CHAPTER TWENTY

AT MY COMMAND, UNLEASH CHAOS ...

One thing I learned from staging my own epic birthday gladiatorial contest is that gladiatorial contests are ROUGH. Even when they're only for pretend. They're still ROUGH.

I blame the chickens.

Even though I had told the chickens just to pretend to attack the gladiators, and even though I am an actual chicken whisperer, the chickens went crazy.

There's no other way to put it.

They piled into Harry, Meg and Jonny, pecking any bit of them they could find, tugging at Harry's tutu, pulling Meg's curly hair, knocking Jonny over and pecking his face.

The gladiators hardly had a chance to pretend-spear them; the chickens were a frenzy of feathers and beaks.

Meg hid under her pan lid.

Harry the Hulk was spinning around, trying to shake off four chickens clinging to his outstretched arms.

Jonny had to hide in the apple tree.

I don't know what they found so funny, but Mr Hector and Nana, watching it all, were chuckling away.

Only Keith was sticking to the brief. He had a megaphone he'd made out of rolled-up cardboard.

'Back in ancient times, back when there were no TVs or PlayStation, Roman people had fun by watching gladiators in the Colosseum, fighting wild beasts,' he bellowed, reading from my script.

A chicken had flapped up into the apple tree and got its head inside Jonny's pyjama trouser leg.

'Here, under the shadow of the mighty volcano Vesuvius, gladiators fight beasts to the death, with the emperor watching,' Keith continued.

Meg was lashing out with her plastic pipe sword from under her pan-lid shield, shouting, 'Take that, you filthy bird!'

'Call them off!' Jonny shrieked from the tree. 'They've gone nuts!'

'Enough!' I shouted. 'Chickens – **CALM! DOWN!'**

And as quickly as they had attacked, the chickens stopped.

Jonny hopped down from the tree, panting a bit.

Meg appeared from under her pan lid.

Harry straightened his tutu.

Everyone was red in the face and sweating.

'Right!' I said. 'Let's take a short break, then we'll try that again.'

'And remind them they need to play nicely,' said Jonny.

'Yeah, or I'll rip them to bits,' said Meg, jutting out her chin.

This was a very un-Meg-like thing to say.

She was obviously quite worked up. This is another thing I've learned about gladiatorial contests – they get people all worked up.

The gladiators straightened up their costumes and grabbed their weapons again. I whistled to the chickens to get ready. Then I yelled:

'Let the games commence – again!'

This time the battle went much better. The chickens were more restrained.

Meg, Harry and Jonny were able to wave their plastic pipe spears.

Some of the chickens pretended to be wounded and did some good broken-wing acting.

At one point, Meg had chicken Caesar pinned to the ground with her plastic pipe sword – it was very dramatic.

I raised my thumb, meaning let the chicken live – I was really getting into the emperor role now – then rushed off to get Tiny from the kitchen.

My plan was to unleash a zebra into the Colosseum for the gladiators to fight – I'm pretty sure they had zebras in real gladiator fights – only Tiny, being Tiny, wouldn't walk straight. She wandered off into the bushes and then lay down in a puddle. I shooed her up. I didn't want the water to smudge her disguise.

Plus, if Nana saw that she was a pig – *the* pig that killed her dog – and not an actual zebra, there would be mega trouble.

Tiny got up and wandered away. It was hopeless. I couldn't waste time trying to steer her back. Most of the chickens had been vanquished now; some had hopped out of the Colosseum to peck the grass.

Mr Hector and Nana were talking quietly together. Keith had tried on Harry the Hulk's tutu and was prancing around in it. The show was losing its direction.

I led Major to the wheelbarrow-slash-chariot. Using some more twine, I tied him to it. He stood between the handles, like a mighty horse that might pull along a mighty emperor – **ME!** – in a golden chariot. I hopped in the back, my feet dangling out, and Major headed straight for the Colosseum.

We made a spectacular sight. I know this because everyone stopped mucking about. I waved in an emperory way. Everyone cheered. Mr Hector and Nana clapped and lobbed little apples at me, which rained down like appley confetti. What a moment!

I tried not to laugh. I didn't want to ruin the emperor effect. But it was hard. I felt so happy. This was so much fun – the best birthday fun you could ever wish for. I wanted this moment to last forever. My friends cheering, apples raining down, me being pulled along in a golden chariot by a mighty dog-horse.

Unfortunately, nothing lasts forever – I have learned this – and as I took another triumphant lap, with the crowd roaring, Tiny, disguised as a zebra, waddled into the Colosseum.

CHAPTER TWENTY-ONE

AN IMPERFECT STORM

'A zebra! A zebra in the Colosseum!' Keith shouted through his megaphone. 'Gladiators, attack!'

They didn't get a chance.

Major looked at Tiny the zebra, sniffed and wagged his tail. I guess you can disguise how a pig looks, but you can't disguise its piggy smell, and Major instantly recognised Tiny. He leaped forward so fast I was thrown out of the chariot. The twine snapped, and Major broke free.

Major bounced around Tiny, scattering chickens and apples as he went.

Keith tried to stick to the script, signalling to Meg to uncover the volcano cake. He raised the megaphone to his mouth and yelled:

'But oh no! What is that noise? What is that rumbling? The mighty volcano Vesuvius is going to erupt!'

Then there was a massive booming sound that seemed to shake the trees. How had Keith done that? Amazing! He truly was all over the special effects.

Then Keith threw some flour over everyone.

'What are you doing?' Nana shrieked, brushing it off her purple loon pants.

'Hot ash rains down from the volcano!' Keith boomed through his megaphone. 'See the ash, raining down!'

There was a bright flash of light and another huge boom. This time everyone looked up.

The booming sound wasn't Keith's sound effects. It was thunder.

I felt a raindrop on my face. Suddenly, lots of fat drops fell from the sky.

'Oh horror! Oh despair! Oh no!' Keith continued. 'Vesuvius is erupting. Run for your lives! The emperor and gladiators and crowd all flee in panic.'

Tiny waddled into the long grass and everyone else sheltered under the apple tree. Everyone except Keith. His cardboard megaphone was soaked and beginning to sag, but he wouldn't be put off.

'Soon boiling lava will flow down from the volcano's sides.' Keith pointed at the volcano cake. Not only was it getting wet, but it was surrounded by chickens, all pecking the strawberry-laces lava off it. Strawberry-laces lava that looked just like worms, if you are a chicken.

'My cake!' Meg cried, shooing the chickens away. 'That took three hours to make!'

Another thunderclap.

BOOM!

'Soon, chunks of hot lava and rock will explode out of the volcano!' Keith went on.

And chunks did rain down.

Not chunks of lava, though.

Bacon sarnies.

Bruce had arrived, but no one had heard him except Major, who had jumped up, whacked the tray Bruce was carrying and sent a shower of sandwiches raining down upon us all.

'My sarnies!' yelled Bruce.

Things got a bit frantic.

We all ran round trying to rescue the sandwiches, while Major tried to eat them all.

The flour on our faces, clothes and hair turned to gummy splodges.

Meg tried to cover up the volcano cake, but the box was soggy and kept collapsing.

Then suddenly, from the bushes, came a squeal and a sound of thundering hooves. The grass parted and a zebra, aka Tiny, came running out at top speed.

I think maybe Tiny had found a stray sandwich and smelt the bacon in it. Bacon is obviously upsetting to a pig. Tiny *was* upset and she was heading straight (for once) at Meg's cake.

Meg managed to grab Tiny's straw mane as she ran past and swing herself up on to Tiny's back. Meg steered Tiny away from the cake, but now they were thundering straight for Nana under the apple tree.

Nana didn't move. Maybe she couldn't move. Her eyes were wide, staring at this creature bombing towards her.

In the downpour, Tiny's zebra disguise was washing off. Her straw tail dropped off, revealing her curly pig one.

Nana put her hand to her mouth. Mr Hector dived towards Nana, pushing her out of the way just as Tiny was about to crash into her.

Nana struggled to her feet.

'That's the pig that killed my dog,' she said. 'And now it's running off with my grand-daughter! After them!'

Then Nana set off after Tiny.

'See the people fleeing from the volcano,' shouted Keith through the megaphone.

I admired Keith for sticking to the script; it showed great resilience. Sadly, though, it was a waste of time. The show was clearly over. We all ignored Keith and chased after Nana.

CHAPTER TWENTY-TWO

THE CHASE

You know those police car chases you see in films, when there's a barrier over the road and the car in front just drives straight through it, smashing it to bits?

That's what Tiny did to Mr Hector's gate.

She was running so fast and just smashed

through the gate. Meg ducked as pieces of wood exploded everywhere.

Nana was running along behind, waving a pipe spear. Then there was me in a kaftan, Jonny in pyjamas and Harry the Hulk wearing his tutu. After a few seconds of stampeding, Keith caught up with us, too. All the chickens were with him.

'This isn't in the script!' he yelled at me.

Thunder boomed overhead. Tiny swerved into a road. Cars slammed on their brakes and honked their horns.

My kaftan was wet and slowing me down, and the soggy gladiators were tripping over pieces of their costumes as they fell apart. Tiny raced into the park and past Bruce's cafe, scattering the people who were queueing up outside. I ran after them – and straight into Dad and Mum.

'Where have you been, Tom? We've been looking for you,' Mum said.

I hadn't told them where I was going this morning for my birthday. They were clearly furious with me.

'We're not furious with you,' said Dad.

Huh??

Confusing.

'The opposite. You're a star, you've saved us!' he went on. 'My pasta sauce, that you gave to Bruce here in the cafe. It's a total sensation. Someone from a big supermarket tasted it and now he wants me to make it for everyone. Tons of it. To sell in all their stores.'

'It's a real job for Dad,' said Mum. 'No more writing a book. It means I can cut back my hours at work and be around for you a bit more.'

'I was never going to finish my book anyway,' Dad said.

'He was never going to finish his book anyway!' Mum laughed.

Yes, laughed.

Quite a mad sort of laugh, admittedly, that went on a bit too long, but at least it was a laugh.

I couldn't take it all in. I said nothing, and they just hugged me. They didn't mention my birthday, but that was OK. It was a good hug.

'This is great news, but Nana's chasing Tiny down the road saying she's a murderer. Plus, Meg's riding her and I'm worried she'll fall off.'

'Riding Nana?' Mum asked.

'No! Riding Tiny. There's no time for explaining. They're getting away!'

We all started running now – Mum and Dad, too. We were shouting at Nana to stop. She couldn't hear us.

'Hold on, Meg!' shouted Keith through his soggy megaphone. 'We're coming!'

Then Major bounded up alongside me, still licking his lips from all the bacon sarnies he must have scoffed in Mr Hector's garden.

Suddenly, I had an idea. I grabbed Major and then called the chickens over. My chicken-whispering skills had been a bit patchy, but they were my only chance. I got the chickens to jump on to Major's back.

'Ride Major until you're alongside Nana, then jump off and surround her,' I said. The chickens nodded.

'Keep her away from the pig-zebra. Use any means possible. Meg is in danger. Go!'

The chickens gripped Major's fur and then, with a huge leap, Major shot down the road. Wow, that dog was fast. He just took off. I half expected the chickens to fall off him, but they clung on.

I pulled my kaftan up and did a final

sprint. The chickens flapped down off Major's back, landing in a line between Nana and the speeding pig. They formed a circle around Nana, wings out.

Nana was panting. Not surprising really. This was probably the most exercise she'd done in about sixteen years.

'Stay back!' she said, waving her pipe spear around. The chickens had their beaks open a bit, ready to peck.

Mum and Dad ran up. Then Jonny, Harry and Keith, Mr Hector and Bruce followed on behind.

'What in the name of **craningfords** is going on?' Dad puffed.

'That's what I'd like to know, too,' said a voice I didn't recognise.

There was a man holding a phone, staring angrily at all of us. He looked a bit familiar.

Then I saw Chas standing next to him and realised where we were.

There was a pond; a statue of a woman in a curtain; a very posh car. Oh great.

We had ended up in the garden of Chas Cheeseman's house. Here was Chas, smirking, and this man was Chas Cheeseman's dad.

'I'm calling the police,' he said.

CHAPTER TWENTY-THREE

WHAT'S ALL THIS, THEN?

It didn't take long for the police to arrive. The officer got out of the car and my heart sank. It was the same one who had come round with Margherita in the pizza box, after I had buried her in the Bright Futures nursery sandpit and the children had dug her up again. I really hoped he didn't mention this.

Mr Cheeseman said a girl riding a zebra had trampled through his garden, followed by Nana and a huge dog being ridden by chickens.

'Can you identify the dog?' the police officer asked.

'Yes, it's that one,' said Mr Cheeseman, pointing at Major, who was licking the police officer's trouser leg. 'And those are the chickens who formed a circle around that lady,' he said, pointing at Nana.

The police officer said he'd never heard of chickens doing something like this.

'Expect you've never heard of a chicken whisperer, then,' said Mr Hector. 'Tell him, Tom, about your powers.'

'I'm a chicken whisperer,' I muttered.

'A chicken what?' said the police officer. 'Speak up, lad.'

'I am a chicken whisperer.' I said. 'I can control chickens. A bit.'

The chickens all clucked and nodded in agreement.

The police officer stared at me, squinting. Then he shook his head.

'And why did you tell the chickens, if that's what you did, to apprehend this elderly lady?' he asked.

'She was chasing my sister,' I said, 'who was riding on our pig. It was dangerous.'

'And where are this sister and this pig then, might I ask?' the police officer said.

'There!' shouted Keith, as Harry and Jonny pointed their plastic pipe spears towards a nearby hedge. Meg was crawling out of it, followed by Tiny.

'That's a pig?' the police officer said. 'Weird markings.'

'It's disguised as a zebra for gladiatorial combat, but the rain has ruined the stripes.' I said.

'Gladiatorial combat?'

'In Mr Hector's garden. That's why we're all dressed up. I was the emperor. Meg, Jonny and Harry were gladiators. Keith was special effects and narrator, and the pig was a zebra. The volcano cake erupted, sending ash which was really flour over us, and Bruce brought bacon sandwiches.

Then Major jumped up and sent all the sandwiches flying and Tiny got spooked by them – pigs get upset by bacon – and ran away. With Meg riding on her back.

Then Nana chased after her, once she realised she was *the* pig that squashed her dog and not a zebra at all. And that's how we came to be here.'

The police officer was staring at me. His mouth was open. He had given up taking notes.

'Is this true?' Dad asked.

'He wanted to arrange something we'd all enjoy and remember,' said Keith. 'So he went for Vesuvius erupting over a gladiator show. With bacon sandwiches.'

'It just got a bit out of hand,' Jonny added.

'Although we looked fabulous!' added Harry the Hulk.

'Tom just wanted a really fun, cool birthday,' said Meg. 'After you cancelled it.'

'Please don't be angry with me,' I said. 'I'm sorry, everyone. It's all my fault. I tried to fix everything but it didn't work. I just wanted my Lucky Birthday. You can arrest me if you like, Officer. I will come quietly.'

I held my two hands out, wrists together, ready to be handcuffed.

The police officer unclipped his handcuffs from his belt and walked towards me. But then he just laughed and said, 'Fooled you, only joking!'

Then everyone hugged me. Literally everyone. I was smothered. And confused.

Nana said she was sorry she had chased Tiny. She said something about forgiveness and said she respected Tiny for freaking out about the bacon sarnies, as she was a vegetarian, too.

Mum said that I had actually fixed my family, without even realising.

'What you have done is make me see just how lost your dad and I got,' said Mum. 'We will never take our eyes off important things like you and your birthday again.'

'Speaking of which,' said Dad, 'isn't it about time we celebrated? Together, all of us. It's your special day!'

'Reckon that means all back to mine!' said Mr Hector. Everyone cheered.

Chas Cheeseman's dad complained about justice not being done, but this was drowned out by the sound of everyone singing 'Happy Birthday' to me.

Then the police officer took me to one side.

'I remember you,' he said. 'You're the one that buried a flat chihuahua in the sandpit of Bright Futures nursery.'

I gulped hard. I felt the colour drain from my face.

Then he grinned.

'Don't worry. We'll let that go, too. In fact, I'll give you a lift in the police car if you like, as it's your birthday.'

Then he let me sit in the front of the police car – an actual real police car. He put the blue lights on and as we drove off I could hear

Chas asking his dad why he'd never had a ride in a police car for his birthday.

Everyone followed: Mum and Dad and Meg, my friends, Nana and Mr Hector (who were now holding hands), Bruce from the cafe, Tiny the pig and Major the dog and all the chickens streaming along behind.

It was, I can safely say, the very best moment of my entire life.

CHAPTER TWENTY-FOUR

WHAT'S A LUCKY BIRTHDAY ANYWAY?

The rest of my birthday was a blur. A happy blur. If I had to list all the good things that happened, it would take ages. So I won't, but here are the highlights:

1. Mr Hector got his fiddle out and played

'country songs from when he was a lad back in his village'. Nana was on maracas. The two of them kept looking into each other's eyes and smiling.

2. Meg took the tutu off Harry the Hulk and danced around all afternoon. I pointed out that she had suggested bunting, riding and dancing when I was planning my birthday and she'd had all of them (if you counted riding on a pig and bunting made of old pants, that is).

3. The police officer, whose name was Mike, started training Major, and Major loved it. 'We could do with a dog like this in the force,' Mike said, and Harry agreed that Major could start a new life as a police dog.

4. Mum explored the whole of the secret garden and began planning ways to grow veg in it with Mr Hector. He said he could really do

with her help. She said she'd love to work in a garden again, after she had given up her allotment years back to work all the time.

5. The cake had survived. It was a bit wet, but it tasted good.

6. Tiny crunched up all the fallen apples that had dropped down in the storm, then rolled around on the grass, wiping off the last of her zebra costume. Nana scratched her tummy.

7. Jonny and Keith pulled Harry round in the chariot, laughing their heads off.

8. The sun came out.

Towards the end of the afternoon, I crept off into the bushes and sat quietly. All the chickens sat in my lap and around me. I thought about the day – my birthday; my Lucky Birthday. What was a Lucky Birthday,

after all? Meg and I hadn't been able to remember hers properly.

We had thought it would be about presents and cool trips and a sleepover, but it wasn't.

A Lucky Birthday was discovering that your best friend, Keith, is a **genius**.

It was about realising that your sister is smart and tough and totally on your team.

And that your mates are so awesome they'll do anything, including dressing up as gladiators and fighting chickens, to make sure you have a great day.

It's about realising that flash presents and fancy parties like Chas Cheeseman had aren't important, but fun and real friends are.

It's about finding a new career for your dad as an ace pasta-sauce maker.

It's about your mum smiling more and working less.

It's about helping your nana feel less lonely, not with a new pet but a new relationship (yes, her and Mr Hector! I know!).

It was a lot to think about. Maybe I hadn't planned all the great things that had come out of this day, but I did somehow make them all happen. So, I guess a Lucky Birthday is also about discovering that you can pull off pretty much anything if you put your mind to it (and visit a DIY store with around £8 in your wallet).

I lifted the chickens out of my lap, straightened my kaftan, and went back to join the party.

'Tom, there you are, we've been looking for you!' shouted my dad. 'Everyone's starving. Let's go back to the house. I spotted just the thing in the freezer earlier.'

Then he turned towards everybody, raised his arms high and shouted, **'WHO FANCIES PIZZA?'**

BORED OF YOUR BROTHER?

SICK OF YOUR SISTER?

READY FOR
A BRAND NEW,
SUPERCOOL SIBLING?

**READ ON FOR AN EXTRACT FROM THIS
LAUGH-OUT-LOUD ADVENTURE FROM**

Jo Simmons

CHAPTER ONE

CLICK!

CHANGE BROTHERS AND SWITCH SISTERS
TODAY WITH
www.siblingswap.com

The advert popped up in the corner of the screen. Jonny clicked on it instantly. The Sibling Swap website pinged open, showing smiling brothers and happy sisters, all playing and laughing and having a great time together.

What crazy alternative universe was this? Where were the big brothers teasing their little brothers about being rubbish at climbing and slow at everything? Where were the wedgies and ear flicks? What about the name-calling? This looked like a world

Jonny had never experienced, a world in which brothers and sisters actually *liked* each other!

'Oh sweet mangoes of heaven!' Jonny muttered.

It was pretty bonkers, but it was definitely tempting. No, scrap that: it was *essential*. Jonny couldn't believe his luck. Just think what Sibling Swap could offer him.

A new brother. A *better* brother. A brother who didn't put salt in his orange squash, who didn't call him a human sloth, who didn't burp in his ear. That kind of brother.

Jonny had to try it. He could always return the new brother if things didn't work out. It was a no-brainer.

He clicked on the application form.

What could go wrong?

CHAPTER TWO

FIGHT, FATE, FORMS

Only a little while before Jonny saw the
Sibling Swap advert, he and his older brother,
Ted, had had a fight. Another fight.

It was a particularly stupid fight, and it
had started like all stupid fights do – over
something stupid. This time, pants. But
not just any pants. The Hanging Pants
of Doom.

Jonny and Ted were walking their dog,
Widget, on the nearby Common. They arrived
at a patch of woodland, where an exception-
ally large and colourful pair of men's pants
had been hanging in a tree for ages. These
pants had become legendary over the years
the brothers had been playing here. There
was a horrible glamour about them. The boys

were grossed out and slightly scared of them, but could never quite ignore them. And so the pants had become the Hanging Pants of Doom, and now, unfortunately, Jonny had just lobbed Widget's Frisbee into the tree. It was stuck in a branch, just below the mythical underwear.

'Oh swear word,' said Jonny.

'Nice one!' said Ted. 'You threw it up there, so you have to get it down.'

Jonny frowned. Two problems presented themselves. One was the fact that the Frisbee was very close to the pants, making the possibility of touching the revolting garment very real. Second, Jonny wasn't very good at climbing.

'Go on, Jonny, up you go,' teased Ted. 'Widget can't wait all day for his Frisbee. Climb up and get it ... What's that? You're rubbish at climbing? Sorry, what? You would prefer it if I went and got the Frisbee, as I'm truly excellent at climbing?'

'All RIGHT!' fumed Jonny, ripping off his jacket. 'I'll climb up and get it. Look after my coat.'

'Thanks!' said Ted. 'I might use it as a blanket. You're so slow, we could be here until midnight.'

Jonny began his climb slowly, as Ted had predicted, and rather shakily, as Ted had also predicted.

'I'm just taking my time, going carefully. Don't rush me!' said Jonny, as he reached for the next branch.

'Spare us the running commentary,' Ted said.

After several minutes, a tiny dog appeared below the tree, followed by its elderly owner, and it began yapping up at Jonny.

'That's my brother up there,' Ted said to the

lady, pointing up. 'He's thrown his pants into the tree again and has to go and get them.'

The lady squinted up. Her dog continued yip-yapping.

'Oh yes, I see,' she said. 'Well, they're rather splendid pants, aren't they? I can see why he wants to get them back. Are those spaceships on them?'

'Cars,' said Ted.

'Very fetching,' said the lady. 'But he shouldn't throw them into the trees again. A magpie might get them.'

'That's what I told him,' said Ted, trying not to laugh. 'Sorry, I better go and help or we'll be here until Christmas. He's like a human sloth!'

With that, Ted bounced up into the tree, pulling himself quickly up its branches and passing his brother, just as Jonny was within touching distance of the Frisbee.

'Got it!' said Ted, snatching the Frisbee and tossing it down to Widget, before swinging off a branch and landing neatly on his feet. 'You can come down now, bro. Unless you really do want to touch the Pants of Doom. You're pretty close, actually. Look! They're just there.'

Jonny made a noise in his throat – a bit like a growl – and felt his face burning bright red. He was shaking with anger and humiliation as he slowly began making his way down.

By the time the brothers banged back into the house, Jonny was speechless with fury. He ran upstairs. He could hear his mum telling him off for slamming the front door, but too bad. He smashed his bedroom door shut too. There! How's that? He was sick of Ted teasing him, sick of being the younger brother. And as for telling that old lady that the Hanging Pants of Doom were *his* ...

Jonny flipped open his laptop and, miraculously, there was the Sibling Swap website telling him that all this could change. What perfect timing. Had the Sibling Swap team climbed into his head and read his thoughts? Who cared?

He read the home page:

SOMETIMES YOU DON'T GET THE BROTHER OR SISTER YOU DESERVE, BUT HERE AT SIBLING SWAP, WE AIM TO PUT THAT RIGHT. WITH SO MANY BROTHERS AND SISTERS OUT THERE, WE CAN MATCH YOU TO THE PERFECT ONE!

His heart began to beat faster.

SWAPPING YOUR BROTHER OR SISTER HAS NEVER BEEN EASIER WITH SIBLING SWAP! SIMPLY FILL OUT THE APPLICATION FORM

AND WE WILL SUPPLY YOU WITH A NEW BROTHER OR SISTER WITHIN TWENTY-FOUR HOURS, CAREFULLY CHOSEN FROM OUR MASSIVE DATABASE OF POSSIBLE MATCHES. OUR DEDICATED TEAM OF SWAP OPERATIVES WORKS 24/7 TO FIND THE BEST MATCH FOR YOU, BUT IF YOU ARE NOT COMPLETELY HAPPY, YOU CAN RETURN YOUR REPLACEMENT SIBLING FOR A NEW MATCH OR YOUR ORIGINAL BROTHER OR SISTER.

Amazing! For the first time in his almost ten years, this website was offering Jonny power, choice, freedom! It felt good! He rubbed his hands together and began filling out the form.

First, there were two options:

ARE YOU SWAPPING A SIBLING?

ARE YOU PUTTING YOURSELF UP TO BE SWAPPED?

'Easy,' Jonny muttered. 'I'm the one doing the swapping. Me. I have the power!' He did a sort of evil genius laugh as he clicked on the top box. By Tic Tacs, this was exciting! Next, the form asked:

ARE YOU SWAPPING A BROTHER OR SISTER?

'Also easy,' muttered Jonny. 'Brother.'

Then:

WOULD YOU LIKE TO RECEIVE A BROTHER OR A SISTER?

Jonny clicked the box marked 'Brother'. Then he had to add some information about himself.

AGE: NINE.

HOBBIES: BIKING, SWIMMING, COMPUTER GAMES, DOUGHNUTS, MESSING ABOUT.

LEAST FAVOURITE THINGS:

- **MY BROTHER, TED (HE TEASES ME ALL**

**THE TIME AND RECKONS HE'S COOL
JUST BECAUSE HE GOES TO SECONDARY
SCHOOL)**

- **BEING NINE (I *AM* NEARLY TEN, BUT
  CAN I HAVE A BROTHER WHO IS YOUNGER
  THAN ME OR MAYBE THE SAME AGE
  PLEASE?)**
- **SPROUTS**
- **CLIMBING**
- **BEING SICK**

Then there was a whole page about the kind
of brother Jonny might like. He quickly ticked
the following boxes: fun; adventurous; enjoys
food; enjoys sports and swimming; likes
dogs. He didn't tick the box marked 'living' or
the one marked 'human'. He just wanted a
brother, so it was obvious, wasn't it?

That ought to do it, Jonny reckoned. His
heart was galloping now. In just three

minutes it was ready to send. He sat back in his chair. 'Just one click,' he said, 'and I get a brother upgrade by this time tomorrow. Friday, in fact! Ready for the weekend!'

Jonny felt slightly dizzy. He giggled quietly to himself. He felt giddy with power! All he had to do was send off the form. Easy! But then he hesitated … Should he do this? Was it OK? Would he get into trouble? Jonny's dad no longer lived with him and Ted, so he might not notice, but what would his mum say? She'd be pleased, Jonny decided quickly. Yes! After all, she was fed up with Jonny and Ted arguing. This was the perfect solution. Then, with a tiny frown, he wondered how Ted might feel about being swapped, but before he could puzzle this out, there was his brother again, shouting up the stairs.

'Dinner, loser!' Ted yelled. 'Let me know if you need help climbing down the stairs.

They *are* quite steep. It could take you a while.'

That was it! For the second time that day, Jonny felt the anger bubbling up inside like a can of shaken Pixie Fizz. Enough! Double enough!

'So I'm the rubbish younger brother, am I? Well, here's one thing I can do really brilliantly,' he muttered and, jutting out his chin, hit the send button.

CLICK!

'Done!' he said, and slammed the laptop shut.

CHAPTER THREE

GONE

Jonny had a strange dream that night. The doorbell rang, and when he answered it there was a new brother on the doorstep. Only it wasn't a boy, it was a tiny squirrel wearing a green suit, eating a cheese sandwich.

Jonny woke with a start, sat up and rubbed his eyes. Then he remembered! He'd done it! He had swapped Ted, and today, hopefully, his new, improved extra-much-better-er brother would arrive.

'You look excited,' his best friend, George, said at school later. Jonny was tapping his pen feverishly on his desk. 'Like, massively excited. What's going on?'

'Just a bit of family improvement,' said Jonny. Then he leaned across so he was really close to George. 'You won't believe this, but I've swapped Ted!' he whispered.

'Swapped him?' asked George.

'Yes! I'm getting a new brother today. Cool, eh?'

'How? On a website?'

'Yes, have you heard of it? There's this Sibling Swap site where they match you up with a new brother or sister. I had to try it! He's arriving after school.'

George stared hard at Jonny, his eyebrows raised, and was about to speak when their teacher, Mrs Flannery, told the boys to stop whispering and concentrate on their spellings.

As soon as the final bell rang, Jonny raced home. His hand trembled with excitement as he put his key in the door. Once inside, he stood still and listened.

'Ted?' he called out. 'You there?'

Silence.

Jonny looked in the living room.

'No Ted in here,' he whispered. 'I'm talking to myself, but never mind.'

He moved down the corridor. 'No Ted in the kitchen! So far, so good!'

Then he bounded upstairs.

'Bathroom?' he said, looking in. 'Ted-free! My bedroom? Yup, also no sign of an older brother.'

Finally, Jonny paused outside Ted's room. His lair, big brother headquarters, the inner sanctum. A sign on the door said BABY BROTHERS KEEP OUT. With a gulp, Jonny ignored it and stepped cautiously into the room.

Empty.

He sat down on Ted's bed and glanced around. He grinned and then put his hand over his mouth like he'd said a rude word. Then he began to bounce, just a little. Then a little more. Then he leaped up on to the bed, shoes on and everything, and jumped up and down wildly, slapping the ceiling and whooping with glee. Finally, he crashed back on to the bed, panting.

'There doesn't seem to be a single Ted in the house,' he said. 'Now, why is that, I wonder? Ooh, hang on, wait a minute. Is it because Ted was so annoying that his brother decided to swap him on the internet? Yes, I think so. And is that same brother now waiting for a Ted replacement to arrive? Yes, that's right!'

BING BONG.

The doorbell rang.

'And here he is!' said Jonny. 'Let the fun brother times begin!'

HEAD TO
www.siblingswap.com
TODAY

... **your future sibling awaits!**

Change brothers and switch sisters!

Sometimes you don't get the brother or sister you deserve,
but here at Sibling Swap, we aim to put that right.
With so many brothers and sisters out there,
we can match you to the perfect one!

So what are you waiting for?
Get SWAPPING!

- Take the quiz to find your perfect brother or sister
- Meet the founder of Sibling Swap
- Download fun activities and games to play with
  (or without) your sibling!

Jo Simmons began her working life as a journalist. She has written lots of brilliant, laugh-out-loud books for children, including the Pip Street Mysteries and the bestselling, award-winning *I Swapped My Brother on the Internet*. Jo lives in Brighton with her husband, two boys and a scruffy, formerly Romanian street dog. Her favourite ever birthday present was an electric toothbrush.

Nathan Reed has been illustrating professionally since 2000. He has illustrated other fiction series including Grandma Dangerous by Kita Mitchell and Sam Wu by Katie and Kevin Tsang, as well as lots of picture books. Nathan lives in London with his wife and two boys and when not illustrating he can often be found watching his beloved football team, Tottenham Hotspur! His favourite ever birthday present was a Nik Kershaw album when he was six (which he still listens to, but shhh ... don't tell anyone!).

SUMMER HOLIDAYS? BORING!
TINY ISLAND? BORING!
A DODO – A WHAT?! YES!

THIS WILL
BE THE WILDEST
SUMMER EVER!

LOOK OUT FOR THIS
LAUGH-OUT-LOUD ADVENTURE FROM

JO SIMMONS

LOOK OUT FOR MORE LAUGH-OUT-LOUD ADVENTURES FROM

Jo Simmons

COMING SOON!